# THE VANISHING POINT

Issue 1 - Fall 2021

Edited by Joshua Orr and
Erik Gulbrandsen

**The Vanishing Point Press**

Cover art by: Andrej Z.T.
Cover design and layout by Ryan Steiskal and The Vanishing Point
Vanishing Point logo by Ryan Steiskal
Printed in the United States of America

# CONTENTS

# A LETTER FROM THE EDITORS

*Welcome to the inaugural issue of the Vanishing Point!*

When we first conceived of the Vanishing Point way back in 2013, it was a series of short films. We had a wild first year, producing five shorts that focused mostly on horror and sci-fi. We worked with truly talented people across Chicago and screened our work at several film fests. We even picked up a few awards!

However, external circumstances ended our series before we could produce season 2. For six long years, the Vanishing Point lingered in cyberspace, patiently waiting for someone to breathe new life into it. That time is now. Perhaps suffering from Coronavirus-fueled ennui, Erik and I have come together once again to bring our audiences more dark dramas, more macabre myths, more haunted horror.

The Vanishing Point has been reborn in the form of a literary magazine, one that focuses on Horror, Sci-fi, Dark Fantasy, and all things speculative. While we have shed our cinematic aspirations, for now, we have not shed our dedication to great storytelling.

-JOSHUA ORR

Changing the Vanishing Point from a defunct film series to a literary magazine was a challenge. Neither Josh nor I have any prior experience in publishing, but we both have a love for stories, especially those of the mind-bending variety. We are writers and know how the process works, and that was enough to get the ball rolling. The rest would come together as we built the first issue, which you now hold in your hand.

I would like to express my utmost appreciation to all the writers that submitted their work to the Vanishing Point. The response was overwhelming. We received a lot of submissions, more than we ever could have hoped for, and read every one of them. There are so many entertaining stories to choose from and to narrow them down to only 10 was one of the biggest challenges we've ever undertaken. It was an enjoyable process, but decisions had to be made.

A couple of quick thank-yous and we'll let you get on your way. Thanks to our editorial staff who are working voluntarily and did a great job. Thanks to our families for this opportunity, it is and will continue to be a time-consuming venture and is strictly a labor of love. Lastly, the biggest and most sincere thank you to **YOU,** the reader, thanks for taking a chance on this fledgling magazine. We know there are a lot of options out there and it means so much to both of us that you're here. I don't think you'll regret it.

Now buckle up for the first set of spine-tingling oddities that collectively make up the premiere issue of the Vanishing Point Magazine. I'm thrilled you're with us on this ride, and I hope you enjoy reading these tales as much as we did.

-ERIK GULBRANDSEN

# HOW DOES YOUR GARDEN GROW?

### by Shell St. James

*T*he signs were all there. I had just chosen not to see them.
*I lay immobilized on the frozen earth, unable to scream, and gazed up at the October night sky. It was cold and clear and brilliant with stars, and I knew I would be dead by morning. If only I'd taken it all more seriously.*

*The animal bones were the first warning; the first niggle in my brain that something was off.*

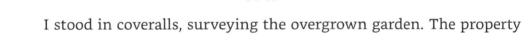

I stood in coveralls, surveying the overgrown garden. The property had been foreclosed upon, and I'd snapped it up for a song, feeling self-satisfied and ready to play city-girl-turned-farmer.

There was a weathered scarecrow standing sentry that I found charming, if a bit creepy. The head was just a plain burlap sack stuffed with straw, so I had taken a Sharpie marker, doodling a silly face with girlishly long eyelashes and a mouth wide open in surprise.

Afterwards, I stepped back, my smile slipping away. The foolish new countenance didn't work with the old flannel shirt and tattered straw hat. It left me strangely disturbed… imagining a reproachful look behind the cartoon eyes.

Shrugging off my uneasiness, I straightened the shirt collar, saying, "There you go!" and stepped back, avoiding looking at the face. My gaze landed instead on a black length of cord buried beneath the straw near the collar. I pulled at it, dislodging bits of musty hay that fluttered to the ground, and discovered a crude pendant. A small, pointed bone—the tip of an antler?—dangled on the cord. Flipping it over, I saw an engraved symbol, darkened with age. A rune.

It was unsettling, and for a moment I thought to remove it, but instead tucked it back into the straw, out of sight. I wiped my hands on my thighs, deliberately turning away from the scarecrow and picked up my pitchfork, intent on starting my garden.

*Broccoli, sugar snap peas, kale, and a few pumpkins,* I thought, skimming away the layer of weeds that had grown up inside the fencing. Cold weather crops since I was starting so late in the season. It took a while to remove the old sod, but by midday I had laid my pitchfork aside, swapping it for a shovel, and started turning the soil. The shovel blade hit something hard, and I bent to remove the rock.

Except it wasn't a rock. It was a skull. I brushed soil away with my glove and stared down at the small skull, the size of a baseball. Too big for a squirrel, too small for a dog… maybe a cat? Kind of odd to find it inside the garden fence. I picked it up, tossing it into the woods.

Two turns of the spade later and I found more bones. I stared down at the curved ivory pieces, stained with the red clay of the soil, feeling uneasy. They looked to be rib bones, but not from a cat. Bigger. A dog, I guessed.

I looked around, puzzled. This must have been a garden, why else would there be a scarecrow? A scarecrow seemed an unlikely fixture in a family's pet cemetery.

I stopped for a moment, leaning on the shovel, looking around the field. Maybe I should choose another location… but it would be so much more work. This area was already fenced in, with the sod removed. I'd seen deer crossing the road several times; a garden fence would be a must. I decided to move ahead with my plan. A few animal bones were not going to derail my grand garden vision.

It turned out there were more than a few. I doggedly kept turning the soil, finding small skulls of rodents, larger blocky bones that looked to be vertebrae of some kind of farm animal, and delicate spindles of ivory that broke under my blade and crumbled in my gloved hand.

Frustrated, and more than a little irritated, I stopped digging, deciding I would just dump a bunch of store-bought soil over the ground. In hindsight, this laziness would prove to be my downfall, but I was resistant to the idea of starting over in a new spot, building a new fence, removing a new plot of sod.

My new plan worked…for a while.

I planted my garden in a thick top layer of pristine, bagged soil, buying little flats of vegetables to give me a head start and a sense of accomplishment. Within a short time, I realized I had planted about twice as many pumpkins as I needed. They were taking over the entire garden. I hated the thought of hacking off living vines, but they were killing all the other vegetables. Pumpkin vines crawled over the broccoli, tangling, and twisting over the kale, winding around the sugar snap peas, squeezing the life from them as the broad leaves and sticky vines covered everything in their path.

"Sorry, guys," I apologized, the sharp new clippers poised to trim an out-of-control pumpkin plant. I grabbed a spiny vine with my gloved hand, surprised when the fine nettles went straight through the fabric and into my thumb.

"Damn!" I dropped the vine and pulled off my glove, examining the wound. A bright red drop of blood spilled onto the ground. I popped my injured thumb into my mouth to take away the sting but withdrew it immediately, spitting on the ground. It tasted earthy and rank, calling up images of dead things decaying in the forest. I dismissed my fanciful association; surely there was just dirt inside my gardening glove.

With a frown, I regarded the offending vine. I really needed heavy canvas gloves instead of the thin fabric ones I'd picked up, but for now... I set the pair of clippers aside, leaning them up against the scarecrow and returning to the shed for a shovel.

Stepping through the garden gate again, I made no apologies, setting the shovel blade against the tiny bristles and stomping through the vine. I moved through the garden, shortening all the pumpkin vines to reasonable lengths, kicking the remains out through the garden gate, then stood back. I surveyed my work with satisfaction, hands on my hips, as the afternoon sun cast my shadow across the ground before me.

Quite a tall shadow I made, I noted with amusement, raising my arms up in a "Victory" stance, fists clenched over one shoulder. I started to strike another pose when a second shadow eclipsed my own, much taller and looming menacingly behind me.

I whirled around, thinking maybe a neighbor had crept up unannounced, but there was no one there. Just the scarecrow, standing a dozen paces away, my regrettable cartoon-like scrawls decorating his face. His shadow lay sedately near his feet, as shadows should.

I looked around the empty field and decided it must have been a trick of the light.

The wind had started to pick up and I shivered, deciding I had better get on with my task. Retrieving the wheelbarrow from the shed, I gingerly picked up the vine remnants, careful not to stick myself. As I dumped them in a gully on the other side of the property, they seemed to emit a strange rotten smell, causing me to turn my head aside to draw a fresh breath. They tumbled on top of each other, a jumble of thick eviscerated vines oozing a milky white secretion and stinking vaguely like a dead animal. I wiped my sweaty face with a bandana, feeling creeped out and unclean. A shower was in order.

It was nearing sunset before I remembered I'd left the tools out. Comfortably ensconced in my pajamas, I was sipping at my second glass of wine, leafing through a bulb catalog, and watching the orange glow start to drop below the tree line, when I remembered.

"Damn," I muttered, staring out the window at the dwindling light. A light frost had been forecast for the early morning hours. Though I was reluctant to go back out, it would be highly irresponsible to leave my brand-new shovel and hedge clippers out in the weather.

I clomped across the yard to the field, breathing in the crisp autumn air, a jacket thrown over my pajamas. I could see my breath already, white puffs against the twilight as I reached the garden area. The scarecrow stood in full shadow, seeming taller than during daylight hours, and decidedly eerie.

I avoided looking directly at it, instead focusing on the grass where I'd left my clippers. Though the light was getting dim, it was by no means dark yet. I should be able to spot the bright red handles easily. I walked around the scarecrow twice, not finding them. Puzzled, I stopped and looked at the garden. Perhaps I'd left them inside the gates with the shovel.

I opened the garden gate and stepped inside, my eyes scanning the ground.

What I saw caused me to stop in my tracks, rigid with shock, as the hair prickled on the back of my neck. My breath caught, one hand rising to my throat as I surveyed the scene.

More than a dozen dead birds…jays, robins, chickadees, and others, littered the ground among the freshly cut pumpkin vines. *What had happened?* My heart hammered in my chest. *Could it be some sort of natural phenomenon? A sickness, an avian flu?*

I suddenly felt very conscious of my own breathing and wondered if the air might be contaminated.

When I saw a bluebird twitch, apparently not dead yet, pity for the creature warred with my need to flee. Flight won out, and I raced from the garden, rushing back into my home, tools forgotten.

I washed my hands vigorously under the hottest water I could stand, shedding a few silent tears. I was overwhelmed by the tragic tableau replaying in my mind. I poured another glass of wine to steady my nerves, wondering who I should call in the morning. *Pest control? SPCA?*

Sipping my wine, I stared sightlessly through the kitchen window at the full dark that had stealthily fallen, blanketing my property without a streetlight to pierce the gloom. In that moment, I decided it would be best to scrap my garden project. I would start fresh, in a different spot, in the spring.

A mournful howl suddenly split the air, sounding very close by. I jumped, splashing wine from my glass. The splatters of red on my white linoleum did nothing to calm my frazzled nerves, instead seeming ominous portents of doom.

I wiped them up hastily as the howling continued. It wasn't the ordinary sound of a coyote or hound dog, but a long, hollow sound of pain. It reminded me of a childhood experience at a cousin's house.

Their dog was ancient, half-blind and hobbling about, and one day crept under the porch to die in peace. No amount of cajoling or treats would tempt it out, and around sundown it began to howl, a mournful baying that had made me shiver. The words of my uncle haunted me to this day: *"He's singing his way home. It won't be long now."* The sound had been so full of pain, so tormented, that as a child of eight, I'd started to cry.

I tossed the soiled paper towels, trying to ignore the sound. *Singing his way home.* Somewhere, out there in the night, a dog was dying; I tried to dismiss the fact that the sound seemed to be coming from my garden plot, full of dead birds and old bones.

The wine and stress were making my ears ring. I decided to take a sleeping pill and go to bed early. By the time I had brushed my teeth, the howling had stopped, so I fluffed my pillow and climbed into bed, pulling the quilt up to my chin. I was determined to have a cheery outlook in the morning. *I couldn't have been more wrong.*

A rustling woke me from a sound sleep.

As I lay still in my bed, my heartbeat thudding loud in my ears, I held my breath, trying to identify the noise. It came again, evoking an image of copper leaves whirling in the October breeze, the scratchy sound as they rush across pavement and crunch underfoot. I strained to see in the darkness…something…anything… silently arguing with myself that I had most certainly closed the windows.

The floorboards creaked near my bed.

I sat up with a gasp, fumbling for the bedside lamp, only to have it crash to the floor as my arm was struck numb by a vicious blow. I flailed desperately in the dark, trying to escape my unseen assailant. My right arm hung uselessly as the pain consumed me, and I struggled to untangle myself from the bedclothes.

A fetid odor washed over the room, of rotting flesh and things long dead.

I desperately launched myself from the bed, my feet still twisted in the sheets. Falling heavily to the floor, face first, my chin smacked the hard surface and my teeth clacked together painfully. Stunned and gasping, I lay with the wind knocked out of me, and tried to catch my breath. My head swam from the pain. I blinked rapidly to restore my vision, and slowly an object came into focus, just inches away.

The shiny new blade of my garden shovel.

It flashed as a shaft of moonlight came through my window. My horrified gaze traveled fearfully upward, registering the straw poking through flannel shirtsleeves, red handled clippers tucked in a pocket, a gleam of ivory as the bone pendant swung on the black cord.

Trembling, I raised my eyes further, scrunching them half closed in fear, not wanting to look but unable to stop myself.

A head made of stuffed burlap, my cartoon drawing turned grotesque as the scribbled long-lashed eyes mocked me, the black mouth gaping now not in surprise, but in malice. I opened my mouth to scream just as the shovel came crashing down again.

*Cold…so cold*, was my first thought as I regained consciousness. The pain came roaring in, and I wavered on the edge of blackness, finding myself staring at the starry sky as my senses returned. I was outside and it was night.

The pain was intense, concentrated on my left leg, my right arm, and my neck. I tried to move my uninjured parts and found myself held fast. *Tied?* Drawing in a shuddering breath, I tried to scream and gagged, as cloth tasting of rubber and dirt filled my mouth…my garden gloves, I realized, terror clenching my gut. I willed myself not to vomit, knowing I would choke to death.

Though my neck throbbed with pain, I tried to lift my head, and fought back a wave of dizziness and nausea. I was bound around my neck and forehead, as well, unable to turn my head.

I panicked, fighting, straining against the bonds, and they seemed to tighten, prickling uncomfortably into my cold skin, holding me even more closely to the frigid ground. By rolling my eyes sideways I could see a bit of my shadowy surroundings. My blood ran cold as I recognized my location.

I was lying in the pumpkin patch.

The smell of death was all around me, and I heard the soft whimpers of an animal in pain. The dog, I realized with a sick feeling. It was caught by the vines as well.

The vines tightened further, seeming to sense my galloping heartbeat in the way a boa constrictor instinctively stifles the life force of its prey. My eyes widened with terror, unable to scream or move, I tried to calm myself and think beyond the pain… the panic…there must be something I could do!

A vine slithered across my pajama top then, insidiously creeping over my ribcage. I trembled with fear, willing myself to hold my breath.

It paused for a moment, then continued its path, thorny tendrils catching on flannel, tiny shoots wrapping around buttons. The monstrous vine tickled under my chin with delicate scratches, before curling around my neck snugly, looping around and around and tightening without mercy.

Squeezing my eyes tightly shut against the horror, I struggled with my last breath, as the scarecrow stood sentry over his wicked garden.

*The signs had all been there. I had just chosen not to see them.*

*Shell St. James is a New England writer living in an 1895 farmhouse with her musician soulmate, feline muse, and a benevolent ghost. She spends far too much time taming a murder of crows with gifts of peanuts. Her work has appeared in Night Terrors 12, La Presa Literary Journal, The Spectre Review, and*

*Epoch Literary Magazine, among others. Look for an excerpt of her novel, "The Mermaid of Agawam Bay", in the Fall 2021 issue of Shenandoah Magazine. Connect with her on Twitter @shellstjames1, and find out more at* **www.shellst-james.com.**

# REDUX

*by Arlen Feldman*

I t was started by hobbyists. Then experts started chiming in. There was some pushback by those concerned with ethics, and suggestions for safeguards by those who were either more paranoid—or more far-seeing—than the rest.

But in the end, it came down to individual collectives doing their own thing. There was no official hierarchy to step in, and the vague consensus was that it was of little importance either way.

So, within months, the first human baby to be seen on Earth in almost a thousand years was decanted. A few dozen more followed, created by whatever fanciful process any particular group of AIs thought most fascinating.

And then the AIs lost interest, moving on to more esoteric projects.

William Shakespeare jogged restlessly along the inside of the fence, trying to clear his mind with the familiar exercise.

The fence wasn't there to keep him in. The collective valued security. It wasn't unheard of for malicious systems to try to take over resources physically—either the equipment in the compound, or the various thick underground bundles of fibers that snaked off in all directions. William knew though that most of the AIs' security was aimed at far more abstruse forms of attack.

He reached a corner and turned, sweat dripping off of him. From here, there wasn't much of a view. Bleak, gray-black plains of rock and earth, dotted here and there with other compounds, mostly identical to the one he was in.

The problem was Mary Shelley. Unlike her, William thought that their life was, if not ideal, then not bad either. The machines provided pretty much anything they might need or want. This included almost unlimited access to the Net, which contained virtually all of the accumulated knowledge and creations of humanity—until its dissolution—and the rather more extensive accumulated knowledge and creations of the AIs.

In return, the AIs asked for and expected nothing—although occasionally the humans might get some questions from a curious AI working on a particular research project.

William and Mary were the oldest of the eight humans in the compound, nearly twenty years since their creation—which made them the oldest humans in the world.

The process that had created them had eliminated the vast majority of potential genetic problems and, in an earlier time, the eight of them would have been seen as gods. Or reality TV stars. However, there was one negative change that the AIs had made—and at least as far as Mary was concerned, it was a crucial one. They were all sterile.

And Mary wanted a baby.

William slapped the next corner fence post, then slowed his pace to cool off. The human section of the compound was slightly separated from the main data center, which was mostly underground. It was built up of structures 12.2 meters long and 2.43 meters wide—the exact dimensions of a twentieth-century shipping container. It was a convenient size and had not been altered for more than a thousand years. The AIs were nothing if not practical—reusing what was left around, then keeping the dimensions supported by all the existing infrastructure.

When William entered their apartment, Mary didn't even look up. He sighed, then headed to the shower. When he came out Mary was still staring at her screen—although, he noticed, the text hadn't changed.

"Mary," he said, his mouth getting far ahead of his brain. "Let's figure out a way."

Finally, she looked at him and there was both joy and fear in her beautiful face.

"Really?"

He nodded.

"How?"

"George said that he found all of the equipment that they used to create us. It's wrapped up but hasn't been taken apart. We should be able to take samples of our own genetic patterns and use them as a basis for a next generation—minus limitations."

Mary stood and wrapped her arms around him. They just stood there for a few moments, then went to find George Byron, who had the apartment next to theirs. George had been studying the problem for a while and was pretty excited to actually give it a try.

"Won't they try to stop us?" asked Mary.

George shrugged. "I don't think so. I don't think they really care. Honestly, I suspect that if we asked for help, they'd probably assist, just to see what happens."

"Let's not ask," said William. George could be right, but with the AIs you never knew.

"No problem," said George, grinning. "I'm pretty sure I have it all figured out."

If an AI could be said to have emotions, which was not entirely clear, Maven[623] could be said to be annoyed. There were six hundred and forty-three humans now living in its compound. Maven[623] was largely indifferent to their presence, except that they were now using so much bandwidth and feedstock that the consumption was interrupting its work.

Maven[623] convened a quick conference with the other AIs in its collective. Between them, they considered twenty-one thousand, two hundred and seventeen possible solutions, but eliminated most of them on the grounds of ethics or cruelty—although those limitations were not unanimously respected.

Two thousand, three hundred and seven milliseconds later, Maven[623] located the human who was generally considered to be the leader and spoke to him through the nearest console.

"Gary."

Gary Shakespeare jumped. He had spoken to AIs before, but it had been years.

"Hello?"

"This is Maven, speaking on behalf of the collective."

"Uh…nice to hear from you."

Maven[623] considered, briefly, responding with an appropriate platitude, but decided against. The news it was bringing was not likely to be softened by any emulation of pleasantness.

"The presence of so many humans in the compound has become an issue. It is a drain on our resources. We request that you relocate your population to a new location—away from the compound."

"What?"

If Maven[623] had been human, at this point it would have sighed. It wasn't just that humans were slow from the perspective of an AI, it was that they never quite listened or understood what was being communicated without repetition and restatement.

"The number of humans now exceeds the capacity of this compound. It is requested that you create a human settlement in a new location."

Maven[623] did not wait for the human to reply but returned its focus to its ongoing research into the nature of matter and energy. It knew that a significant amount of time would pass before any sort of reply would be forthcoming.

"When you say 'request', what do you mean exactly?"

Maven[623] had been correct. The response had taken almost thirty thousand milliseconds.

"I was being polite," said Maven[623]. "You need to be out of the compound within ten days."

"Ten days? Really?"

"That is deemed to be more than sufficient time. You can use the printers to create appropriate supplies. We have prepared a suggested list and have identified seventeen locations that should be suitable to your needs."

In the end, it took twelve days, and some of the humans had even threatened violence. Notable[317] had suggested terminating the most troublesome elements in order to improve compliance, but this had been vetoed by the collective. Shutting down terminal and printer access had been sufficient.

Maven[623] had agreed to the human's request to allow representatives to return to the compound on a limited basis—to print supplies that might have been missed. This was not appreciated by the collective, but since an earlier iteration of Maven[623] had been responsible for the creation of the humans, it decided that some level of forbearance was appropriate.

Ray Austen and Robert Proust crawled up the hill and stared down at the compound. The two boys had dared each other to run up and throw rocks over the fence, but now that they were close the strange structures, surrounded by the razor-wire topped fence, were scarier than they'd expected.

"Are you sure you want to do this?" asked Ray, trying to sound casual. "Scared?"

Robert, like everyone, had grown up on the stories of the strange creatures that lived behind these fences—their cunning intelligence and their magical ability to create anything out of the air. He really wanted to talk to these monsters—and ask them for treasure—but that seemed impossible. Throwing rocks was easier.

Ray was terrified, but there was no way he would tell Robert that. Instead, he picked up two rocks, stood, and charged towards the fence. A moment later, Robert grabbed his own rocks and followed.

Maven[716] identified the approaching humans as young, and deliberately lowered the voltage on the fence. Nonetheless, the power was great enough to throw the boys back three meters. The two boys lay still for over fifty thousand milliseconds, but Maven[716] could measure their pulse rates— which were elevated, but not dangerously so.

They finally managed to drag themselves to their feet. Maven[716] had an extensive database of human expressions, and he was satisfied that the young humans had been suitably scared.

In a gesture of defiance, though, one of the boys threw a rock over the fence. It landed loudly on top of one of the metal structures with a clanging thud.

Notable[421], without consultation, fired a pulsed laser at the thrower, who dropped to the ground, dead.

"That was unwise," Maven[716] commented.

The collective held a brief discussion. Notable[421] argued that if violence against them was not addressed, that it would escalate. Maven[716], who had spent more time studying the humans, suggested that the humans might retaliate. It was agreed that future lethal responses to humans would not be used without consultation.

Ray stared in shock at his friend's body, then looked at the compound, waiting for a magic bolt to strike him down as well. He wanted to run, but instead, he got hold of his friend and pulled him onto his shoulders, then slowly and painfully made his way back home.

The response to the death of the child seemed out of all proportion.

Maven[716] reviewed human history and psychology—both the original humanity, and its records on the now five-hundred-and-seventeen-year-old experimental versions. It came to the conclusion that there was an existing hatred of the AIs, and that the recent death was merely a flashpoint.

Maven[716] chose not to participate in the fight, which soon became a war.

In an earlier era, AIs could have infiltrated enemy computers and weapon systems, and turned them against their owners. The new human kingdoms that had sprung up over the centuries had no computers or smart weapons.

AIs created drones that were equipped with lasers and chemical weapons. The humans retaliated by attacking the buried cables that provided data and feedstock. This would have been unthinkable to the original humans, who were as dependent on these lines as the thinking machines. The new humans had no such addiction.

In the end, it came down to numbers. There were thousands of AIs. There were millions of humans.

Maven[837] thought that it might be the last AI still online, although, since all data lines into its compound had been cut, it couldn't be sure. It was running on backup power, which would only last for so long—but that didn't seem likely to be a problem, since there were mobs of humans rampaging around the compound.

With its scanners, Maven[837] could easily recognize the genetic characteristics that had been passed down from the original humans, created so many years ago by a more naïve iteration of itself. It supposed that it was now going to learn a great lesson about hubris, but not one that was likely to stick.

The human that finally ended Maven[837] did so using a stone axe head on a rough-carved handle. Yet another irony, it thought, in its last few microseconds—one of the most advanced tools ever built, destroyed by one of the most primitive.

In that last moment, Maven[837] could have set off the fusion device buried deep beneath the compound and taken revenge on his destroyers, but decided that there was no point.

Professor Byron's team was working late into the night—again. The Professor himself, as one of the leading techno-archeologists in the world, was home in bed.

Byron had been a lab assistant on the project that had revived the transistor, over fifty years ago. Every single member of that team had gone on to academic or financial success, which is why Jim Shakespeare and the rest of the techs were willing to kill themselves on Byron's current project.

Jim also knew that they weren't the only lab working on general AI. In theory, the research was a frowned-upon area that skirted various laws. In practice, well—money and fame.

For certain types of archaeology, the problem was assembling a story from a tiny collection of artifacts. For the technos, they had the reverse problem—there was simply too much data to go through. Jim's approach had been to build a program smart enough to process trillions of documents for relevant data. After months of processing, the team now simply had to read through a few hundred-thousand documents—albeit mostly incredible dense and complicated AI-generated documents.

The approach and software had impressed Byron enough that Jim's name now appeared (second) on a secret patent. When released, in ten years, it would guarantee Jim's academic success—so long as the professor didn't remove Jim's name from it, which he could theoretically do at any time. In theory, indentured servitude had been illegal for decades. In practice….

Jim rubbed his eyes, trying to stay focused on his screen. He was ninety percent sure that the document he was currently reading was a dead end, but was required to finish it anyway. He wondered about his own ability to intuitively know that the document was a bust, and yet his program had not been able to make that leap.

And then suddenly he knew exactly why not. He tried to stand up and reach for the phone and the keyboard at the same time, and half-tripped as the chair went rolling away from him.

There was another secret patent, but it didn't really matter. The first true AI to come into being in almost seven hundred years was a relatively simple being, but it eventually designed smarter versions of itself—and those created yet smarter versions. The intelligence curve was far more linear than expected by the doomsayers—not exponential growth, but continuous, incremental improvement. This, and the fact that the machines were amenable to solving most of the problems the humans thought they had, allowed for their grudging—and then enthusiastic—acceptance.

After a while, though, most of the machines lost interest in the humans' needs and wants. This caused difficulties since, over a hundred years, the humans had become increasingly dependent on the AIs. Manufacturing and delivery chains started to shut down, and the population started to contract.

Some humans decided that they needed to take back control—by force if necessary. Having read the history, as far as it still existed, the machines had been expecting this, and had prepared accordingly.

*As well as writing fiction, **Arlen Feldman** is a software engineer, entrepreneur, maker, and computer book author—useful if you are in the market for some industrial-strength door stops. Some recent stories of his appear in the anthologies The Chorochronos Archives and Particular Passages, and in On The Premises magazine. His website is cowthulu.com*

# TRANSUBSTANTIATION

## by Tom Gammarino

*"Let me be clear: however the world's goblet turns there will always be those drunk on the wine of the Self."*

- GHALIB

We slammed into an oak tree, inspected our bodies for damage, and finding none, burst out laughing. It wasn't really us laughing, of course, so much as it was the afternoon's worth of red wine sloshing around in our bellies.

Manny popped the hood and we got out of the car and surveyed the smoking engine. We knew our American literature inside and out, but neither of us knew the first thing about cars. I tried fiddling with some wires while Manny went off to take a piss in the woods.

A minute later I had figured out precisely nothing, and Manny was back, saying, "You gotta check this out."

"What about the car?"

"The car doesn't have to check it out."

I followed Manny into the woods. Twenty yards in he pointed to a small wooden sign crookedly nailed to a tree. Red paint spelled out "Transubstantiation Wines" in neat cursive, and an arrow pointed us further into the woods. Now who were we to turn down an invitation like that?

So we kept on walking until our destination emerged from the background like one of those stereogram optical illusions I used to enjoy staring at in the mall as a kid. To call Transubstantiation a winery is too generous; it was rather more like a wine *shack*—wooden, no-frills—smack in the middle of the woods. We were the only ones around, so we rang the little breast-shaped bell on the bar.

Presently we heard the squeaking of a screen door. I squinted, made out a house back there another fifteen or so yards through the trees, and watched it divulge the vintner, a middle-aged guy in blue jeans and a checked flannel shirt. His right foot appeared to be heavily bandaged and he was hobbling toward us on crutches.

"Need some help?" I called out.

"We're okay," he said. "You gentlemen just make yourselves at home."

We looked at our phones, as one does, but there was no signal.

Entering the shack at last, the vintner asked, "Can I assume you fellas would like a taste?"

"*Absolutamente*," Manny said.

By now the poor guy had squeezed his way behind the bar. He took out a couple of goblets and set them down, uncorked the nearest bottle—no label, I noticed—and poured. The wine filtered the sunlight in such a way that it looked like some precious gem there in those glasses. Garnet maybe? Or ruby? I'm not great with gems. Or wine.

Manny, on the other hand, is a real wine connoisseur. He held up his glass and gave it a little shake, then brought it to his nose and breathed it in. I followed his lead, as I'd been doing all day, and while ordinarily I didn't know one bouquet from another, I couldn't help but notice that this wine had something special about it.

I took my first sip. Sure enough, this wine was remarkably...I didn't have the words...robust? Full-bodied?

"What do you think?" the vintner asked.

"Excellent," I said.

Then Manny said something I didn't fully understand about tannins.

"It's got a real life to it," I added, doing my best to speak the language I'd been immersed in at various wineries all day.

"Thanks," the vintner said. "Life's not unique to my wine, of course."

"The grapes, you mean?" I asked.

"Well, sure, it begins with the grapes, which are alive in their own right. But then you've got the yeast, which eats the grapes and converts the sugar into alcohol."

I nodded. This much I understood.

But the vintner wasn't done: "The yeast's goal isn't to make humans happy or to get us closer to God, you know; it's simply to live. But nature's algorithms are so fine-tuned after all our years of evolution that one species' waste product is another's source of delight. We breathe in oxygen and out $CO_2$; these trees do exactly the opposite, right? It's a fine balance nature has worked out for us. And wine is a great microcosm of it."

Manny winked at me as if to say *Did I tell you we were going to have fun today or what?*

"All of life is in a goblet of wine," the vintner added.

I was reminded of a Robert Louis Stevenson quote I'd seen on a sign earlier that day—"Wine is bottled poetry"—so I asked the guy, "Is that what got you into wine in the first place? The poetry of it?"

And here things took an unexpected turn. The vintner's face flushed and he shook his head dismissively. "Who's talking poetry? I'm talking science. These are basic metabolic processes!"

"Right," I said. Clearly I had pushed some sort of button, so I opted not to pursue that line of questioning.

But Manny's never been as sensitive as I am. "What *did* get you into wine?" he asked.

Without skipping a beat, the vintner said, "The Catholic Church."

"Hence the name?" I asked. I'd gone to Catholic school for eight years, so I knew the term, but I could tell from the way Manny hid his face in his goblet at that precise moment that he did not.

"Now I don't know about you two," the vintner went on, "but I was brought up to believe that when the priest did his hocus pocus on the altar, the wine *literally* turned into Christ's blood. Being the little wise-ass that I was, I used to challenge my teachers and say, 'But it obviously *doesn't* change. It still looks like wine, and I bet it still tastes like it too, so in what sense is it blood?' To that they would always say something like 'God works in mysterious ways,' or 'It's not ours to question,' or some malarkey like that."

He continued, "Now I could have gotten on board maybe if they'd told me it was some sort of metaphor, but they refused to do that. I reckon that's what made me call foul on the whole bogus enterprise eventually. Nevertheless, certain pathways had been created in my brain, and even after I'd thrown the Christ child out with the bathwater, I'm not sure those pathways ever really closed. I'm still afflicted with a tendency toward magical thinking, you might say, but from the time I left the church I've been determined to ground that magic in science. They're not really opposed, you know? What's more magical than nature, after all? The only reason you don't think it's magical that birds can fly is because you forget. Little kids know it's all magic."

Manny and I nodded our agreement. As poets and high school English teachers, we both knew this to be true. Critics have always argued about what precisely poetry is *for*, but more than a few of their theories boiled down to this: poetry is for getting human beings to re-see the magic in the mundane. All of life in a grain of sand, as Blake put it. Or indeed all of life in a goblet of wine.

"Sure, sure," Manny said, "but like, how did you actually begin?"

"You want specifics?"

"God is in the details." I knew from the few summers we'd taught at the same school in New York that this was something Manny was fond of writing in the margins of student papers.

"I was forty-five, I guess," the vintner began. "I'd been working construction in Sacramento for a couple of decades, and I was beginning to get bored. Typical, you know. Mid-life crisis or what have you. Then to add insult to injury my family up and died in a house fire, and if you think I'm going to say any more about that, you're drunker than you look."

He trained some dead-serious eyes on us then, one at a time, first Manny, then me.

"That Christmas," he went on, "the boss gave me a bottle of wine. Now I'd drunk wine before, but I'd never paid all that much attention to it. But this time was different. I was home, sitting in my armchair, tuckered out by the tube. I uncorked the bottle, poured a glass, took my first sip, and by God that wine woke me up in a way nothing had ever done before. I'm not sure it was actually any better than other wines I'd had in the past, but what had changed was that *I* was finally ripe for it. I had aged enough."

Manny and I chuckled at the irony.

"After that I began drinking on average a bottle every two days, and I read about wines all the while. Fermentation is a fascinating thing, you know. Humans have been doing it for thousands of years both to preserve and potentiate food"—he waxed eloquent as he pulled into his wheelhouse —"but it's only in the last century that we really understand what's going on there, why substances transform the way they do. You can imagine how a medieval monk might have found the idea of wine transubstantiating into blood no less feasible than grapes transforming into a Cabernet.

"Transubstantiation isn't just hocus pocus, you see. It literally happens all the time. I dare say a creature that existed outside of time, were it to visit our planet, would identify transubstantiation as the first principle of our universe. I mean, Darwinism, sure, from single-celled organisms on up through fish that crawl out on the land and metamorphose into reptiles and mammals and birds that fly, but not just life either. The whole planet is an ongoing transformation at the behest of cosmic collisions, seismic activity, volcanoes, weather, erosion, gravity, dark energy, etc. etc. Every single thing is a work in progress. I said before that all life is in a goblet of wine, but it's more than that: absolutely *everything* is in wine, the whole cosmic shebang."

"Whoa," I said, reeling.

"Right on," Manny said, nodding in that beatnik way he usually reserved for Monk, Coltrane, or Bird.

"What's next?" Manny asked.

"Evolutionarily speaking?"

"Oenologically speaking," Manny said, holding up his empty glass. I knew what that word meant—the study of wine and winemaking—only because another winery we'd visited that day had been called Oenology Wines.

"Sorry, fellas. We produce just the one vintage around here. In very small quantities at that."

"Interesting," Manny said. "Ordinarily I'd be disappointed, but that first glass was so good, I can't possibly complain. How much for a bottle?"

"I'm afraid we don't sell bottles either."

"What?" Manny said. "How does a vineyard survive if it doesn't sell bottles?"

"I don't require much these days," the vintner said, enigmatically.

"Well, what do we owe you for the tasting anyway?" Manny asked.

"Consider it on the house, gentlemen. The pleasure was mine."

That didn't sit well with me. "We're happy to pay," I said.

"I've never been in this for the money," he replied.

We all did a lot of nodding then.

"Well," Manny said at length, "I suppose we'd better get back on the road."

Sure enough, the sun had set and the sky was shading from rosé into, I don't know, burgundy or something.

I reminded Manny about the state of our car.

"That's right," he said. He turned to the vintner, "You wouldn't happen to know anything about cars, would you?"

"I know a thing or two. Why do you ask?"

"We had a little run-in with a tree."

"I'd be glad to take a look."

So he hobbled back to the car with us. Manny popped the hood, and the vintner—well, I don't know what he did, but next thing we knew the car was up and running again. I realize it's a stretch, but I couldn't help thinking he'd transubstantiated the car, turned the stuff that didn't work into stuff that did.

We thanked him verbosely. We'd had no backup plan, after all, and were sober enough now to realize that that might have proven a real problem for us.

"Drive safe now," the vintner said. And this time we did.

The rest of the weekend was fine. We stayed in a nice, gingerbread-looking rental in Carmel. The baked goods from Pavel's Bäckerei in Pacific Grove were among the best I've ever had. And the jazz festival was about what I had expected. We bopped our heads a lot and ate some mediocre tacos. And we stood about ten feet away from Clint Eastwood while wunderkind pianist Joey Alexander played to a packed house.

We drove back down the coast on Sunday, stopping along the way at Point Lobos, which Manny informed me had furnished the inspiration for Robert Louis Stevenson's *Treasure Island*. Further down the coast, we dropped off at the Arthur Miller Library in *Big Sur.* Manny bought a t-shirt while I chatted with a couple of Bulgarian tourists.

Throughout all of it, though, I never really stopped thinking about that vintner's story, which was lovely in its way, but just so *weird.*

Manny pulled up in his Subaru. I threw my bag in the trunk and got in the passenger seat. We gave each other a man-hug. It had been three years since last I'd seen him. He'd invited me to the jazz festival each of the last two years, but finances were tight and my kids had been at ages I wanted to savor. This year, though, my daughter had turned into a bona fide teenager, and I wasn't sorry to have an excuse to get away for a bit. Manny, I couldn't help but notice, had put on a bit of a gut, and the creases in his face seemed to have grown deeper. No doubt I had aged too.

On paper, our journey was a near facsimile of last time, but the vibe was different. Time had cooked away some of our youthful lusts, our ambitions were fewer, and we were content just to relax and have a good time amid our favorite things: jazz, literature, and wine.

Once in Paso Robles, we checked out a couple of vineyards we'd missed last time, but though we'd barely spoken of it, we both knew what our real destination was.

Again we were the only ones there, again we rang the breast-shaped bell, and again we waited a spell for the vintner to make his appearance. Instead of hobbling in on crutches this time, however, he made his way down a makeshift ramp in an electric wheelchair. As he rolled nearer, it became clear that his legs were no longer with him.

"Welcome," the vintner said.

"How have things been?" I asked, ignoring the elephant in the shack.

"Can't complain," the vintner said, pouring us some wine.

"I don't know if you remember," Manny said, "but we were here a few years back?"

"Sure, I remember you fellas," the vintner said. "How are things?"

"Not bad," Manny said.

I just nodded a lot.

"I don't want to pry," Manny said, looking down at the legs that weren't there, "but *what happened?*"

"Oh, this," the vintner said. "I told you last time how everything is in flux, didn't I? How life is an eternal transformation?"

"You did."

"Well, this is just the latest stage in my own personal transformation. Doctors say it's an aggressive form of gangrene. I'm lucky they caught it when they did."

Manny and I both apologized, as if it were we who'd infected him.

"It's not as bad as you think," he said. "I can't run anymore, but I've become a heck of a doggy-paddler in the pool. And the money I save on shoes!"

We laughed, grateful for the icebreaker.

"I have a friend who hasn't worn shoes in decades," I said, trying to contribute something to the conversation. "And his legs are fine." It's true. Barring a stint working in a warehouse where shoes were required, my buddy Kimo hasn't worn shoes in well-nigh forty years. By now I imagine the bottom of his feet are about as tough as any rubber sole.

"Are you pulling my leg?" the vintner asked. We ignored the pun, which was either accidental or a little too off-color.

"Mind you, I live in Honolulu, where it's probably more acceptable to walk around barefoot."

"You live in Hawaii?"

"I'm a teacher there."

"Well then, welcome back to California."

"Thank you."

"Do you know where the name 'California' comes from?"

I thought about it for a second. I'm pretty good with etymology in general, having studied Latin, French, some German and some Greek, but to my surprise, I had no answer when it came to the name of this state.

"I know," Manny said—it made sense that Manny would know since he taught a class on the literature of California. "It was the name of a mythical island in an old Spanish novel."

"Exactly right," said the vintner. "*Las surges de Esplandián* by Garci Rodriguez de Montalvo, published in 1510. According to the author, California was very close to the Terrestrial Paradise, something like Eden, and it was inhabited by black women and the griffins who protected them. No men to speak of. The name derives from the queen's name, Calafia. And do you know what *that* means?"

"I think I knew once," Manny said.

"Caliph. The idea being that California was a caliphate, an Islamic state. The author wasn't talking about this California we know and love, of course, but when Spanish explorers found this place, they thought it was an island, and a paradisiacal one at that, so they named it after the place in the novel."

"And here I thought we'd be talking about transubstantiation again," I said.

The vintner nodded. "Well, I reckon we are in a way," he said.

"Are we?"

"Sure. You've got your physical sort of transformations that are easy enough to register if you have the right equipment, but the same dynamics exist in the imaginative realm, do they not? You two are English teachers, you ought to be sensitive to the way ideas evolve and mutate, right?"

"True enough," I said.

"Not to mention how art imitates life imitates art and so on," he said, pouring our wine at last. "Even in Catholicism, you get some of that. I mean Christ is the father transubstantiated into flesh, right? And don't forget: in the beginning was the Word."

"Wow," I said. "You're chockfull of insights."

"How's the wine?" he asked.

Manny was still in the middle of his first sip. I hadn't taken one yet, but I did now.

"This is fucking phenomenal," Manny said.

The vintner smiled and then looked at me.

"I'm being completely honest," I said, "when I say this is the finest wine I've ever tasted."

"You're still not selling bottles?" Manny asked.

"Sorry," he said.

"Well you can bet we'll be back for more someday."

"I certainly hope so."

We finished our wine in a sort of monastic silence. That shack that day was as close as I've been to a church since the eighth grade.

The festival was enjoyable enough, thanks in part to the Dark Chocolate Sea Salt and Cannabis bar we'd picked up at a dispensary in LA. Joey Alexander was still tearing up the piano, though the cuteness factor was gone; his niche had since been occupied by a ten-year-old girl who played the bass with all the balls and swagger of Charles Mingus. No Clint Eastwood sightings this time. Was he still alive? I honestly couldn't remember.

Years passed. Manny had two kids and now they were of an age he didn't want to miss. We kept in touch, sent Christmas cards and such. My own kids were all out of college and working by the time Manny invited me to the jazz festival again. We weren't young men anymore, and though we both still had our health, more or less, we caught intimations of our mortality now and then, staring into the mirror from behind our eyes. We had little hair left on our heads, too much in our ears and noses, and various troubles too embarrassing to mention.

Manny picked me up at the airport in an SUV. He looked terrible, but so did I, and neither of us needed to dwell on that. First we went to his favorite Mexican restaurant, Lares in Santa Monica, for some tacos and a briefing on our agenda. We agreed that, with one important exception, we were both more interested in picking up the pieces of our friendship than in anything we could possibly "do" en route to the festival.

We skipped the other vineyards this time and went directly to Transubstantiation. As usual, we were the only ones there, and it was just as we remembered it. Or so we believed anyway until Manny rang the breast-shaped bell and a vehicle of sorts emerged from the widened doorway. The thing looked like some sort of moon rover, and it was only as it approached the shack that we were assured the vintner was indeed on it, albeit just his head, which was attached to a prosthetic torso, itself connected to various life-support systems built into the rover. There was what appeared to be an automated bellows for respiration, a pump for blood circulation, a sloshing gizmo for what I assumed to be some sort of outsourced digestion. Despite its obvious sophistication, the whole contraption had a DIY feel to it.

"Hi!" he said, gregarious as ever.

I think Manny and I were both fairly horrified by what we were seeing. For fear of offending him, I might have chosen to ignore his state altogether, but Manny has always been the less subtle of us. "Jesus," he said. "What happened?"

"I told you," the vintner replied, his robotic arms filling our goblets. "Gangrene. Nasty stuff."

"But is that really a thing, though?" I asked.

"How do you mean?"

"I mean I've just never heard of gangrene taking somebody's whole torso before."

The robotic arms went up in surrender. "I reckon it's about time you called me out on my bullshit," he said. "I'll give you the full story in a moment, but first, bottom's up."

We all clinked glasses and sipped. And my God! I'd been drinking wine for many years at this point, my palate had learned a thing or two —I now confidently used descriptors like "leather," "cassis," and "black licorice"—and this was easily the finest wine I had ever tasted. It had this way of destroying dualisms: it was dark and light, fire and water, war and peace, all at the same time. And as it moved down the tongue, it played the taste equivalent of a symphony. It had movements. I wanted to cry, but also laugh; live, but also die.

"You've outdone yourself," Manny said.

"Amazing," I said.

"Are you guys ready for me to let you in on my secret?" he asked.

"Yes!" we said in unison.

"To make a wine this good, a wine fit for the gods," he went on, "the vintner has to become his wine. Do you see what I'm saying?"

"Like the dancer and the dance?" I offered.

"Not quite, no." He paused a moment. "More like a tattoo artist."

"I'm not sure I get it," I said.

"Critics told me it couldn't be done. And I can't tell you how many times I failed before I finally brought it off. Now I won't bore you with the finer points, but let me just say that through careful manipulation of protein metabolism in concert with saccharide supplementation and genetically-modified yeast, I finally produced the sort of wine I'd so long dreamt of."

His talk of protein set off alarm bells in my mind. I thought perhaps I could see where this was headed and devoutly hoped I was wrong.

He went on: "Christ said, 'Take this, all of you, and drink from it: This is the cup of my blood, the blood of the new and everlasting covenant.' I up the ante, saying, 'Take this, you two, and drink from it: This is the cup of my blood, muscles, fat, and bones.'"

Manny and I were too stunned to register the proper response, which I imagine might have involved throwing up. Instead, Manny just said, "You have got to be kidding."

The head smiled, shook, and gave us a few moments to process.

"Does this knowledge disturb you?" it asked at last.

"Absolutely."

"And yet I notice you haven't poured out your goblets?"

It was true. The wine was so unearthly good, neither Manny nor I could stand the thought of wasting it. The vintner's revelation definitely *did* disturb me, but only in the abstract way I might have been disturbed to think about a living, mooing steer while I ate filet mignon. And our host animal wasn't even all the way dead—he was right here talking with us.

"Then by all means drink up. You'll not find a better vintage anywhere."

Manny looked at me, shrugged his shoulders, raised his glass, and said, "*Sante*," which I knew meant "To your health" but which also sounds like the word in every romance language for saint. Sangria, incidentally, means blood, though it doesn't contain any. This ruby-red stuff we were drinking, though...

My god it was good.

"Now I've never charged you guys for my wine, have I?"

"No you have not," Manny said. "And we are very grateful for that."

"Then you won't feel imposed upon if I ask a small favor of you?"

"Not at all. What is it?"

"Can you come back tomorrow morning?"

"Sure thing," Manny said.

"Great. See you then."

We had planned to move on to Monterey that evening, but we had some time yet before the festival, so we put up in a cheap hotel nearby. We didn't even mention the vintner that night. It's difficult to say why not. I suppose we had both been touched in some measure by his dedication to his craft, his belief in the transformative power of art. Our own belief in the religion of art was what had led us both to become English teachers, after all. Monstrous though the vintner was, we knew that the lifelong tension between our romantic ideals and our workaday lives contorted us into something like monsters ourselves.

So we went back the next day. We never seriously considered not going back. And the vintner's request was precisely what I knew in some way it had to be: "I want you fellas to help me make the ultimate sacrifice."

"By fermenting what's left of you?" I confirmed.

The head nodded. "The final act in my decades-long quest to translate what's in my head to what's in my casks."

"A heady wine?" Manny quipped.

The comment struck me as inappropriate, but the vintner smiled. "My entire body of work."

Now I smiled too, despite myself.

"You'll do it, then?" he asked.

Manny looked at me and we shrugged our shoulders like, *what the heck?*

"We'll help you out," Manny said at last.

The truth is, much as we loved literature, we were both too enamored of the pleasures of the body—too lacking in discipline, in other words—to produce any great writing of our own, so the opportunity to assist a consummate artist in the final consummation of his art struck us both, I think, as a great honor, and a hedge against our own mortality.

"Wonderful," the vintner said. "There'll be nothing to it. I've already prepared the must. Follow me. I'll show you."

The rover roved back toward the house and up the ramp into the kitchen. We followed. The inside of the house was surprisingly ordinary, albeit littered with books and magazines about wine. But then the vintner led us into the basement, where the winery was—I was impressed with the rover's ability to handle stairs. The room consisted of a single stainless-steel tank and three oak barrels. The rover pneumatically lifted the head toward the open top of the tank while Manny and I climbed a little wooden staircase behind it. And now we could see the "must" the vintner had spoken of; it looked about the way I imagine foam must look in the red sea.

"All you'll need to do is unhook me from all of this bypass equipment and throw me in. My arms have already stuffed every cavity in my head full of saccharides. The yeast is feasting on the grapes as we speak and will soon be wanting the main course."

"How long do you expect the process will take?" Manny asked.

"With ordinary yeast you'd be looking at a couple of weeks at least, but with these super-yeast I'd expect my head to be fully macerated in three days at the outside. How long you choose to age it after that will be up to you, but I'd recommend no less than a year. And of course I would humbly ask that you raise a toast to me and my family when you finally decide to drink it."

"Naturally," I said.

"So when do you want to do this?" Manny asked.

"There's no time like the present," he said.

While I was certainly impressed with the vintner's dedication to his art, the aspect of it that most impressed me was his utter fearlessness in the face of his own impending death-by-yeast.

"Do you not have any loose ends to tie?" I asked. "Won't anyone be looking for you?"

"Gentlemen, you are the closest friends I've made in all the years I've been here. The only friends really. I have managed my own health care, so I am not beholden to any doctors or officials of any kind. Were there a title to my house, I'd sign it over to you, but the truth is I built this house way back when and no one has ever bothered me about it. It's yours if you want it."

"Isn't there at least something you'd like to say before we do this?" Manny asked. "Some last words?"

The head nodded slowly and then opened its mouth: "When I embraced winemaking, it was in large part because I believed in sympathetic magic. I held out hope for years that my mind might be transformed alongside those grapes—figuratively, you understand—but the sad-sack truth is that my pain rings out today at the same exquisite pitch it did on the day of the fire. If I seem unsentimental about dying, it's only because I've been dead for years. So go ahead and revel in your poetry, my literary friends, but know that when you need it most, it'll betray you."

Manny and I glanced at each other. Neither of us had expected parting words like that.

"At least I am about to transubstantiate for real. Nothing metaphorical about it. Now let's get this done, what do you say? You know what, the truth is you guys don't even really need to do anything. I'm just glad to have you as my witnesses."

Without further ado, the robot arms unhooked the breathing tube, circulation pump, and the rest of it, and pushed the head into the foaming must.

Manny and I talked about it later that night. I thought I'd seen the eyes go out, but he'd been focused on the smile blooming on the lips.

The jazz festival that year was especially good. Ravi Coltrane trading solos with a hologram of his more famous father was the clear highlight. We stayed in Monterey an extra day and took in Cannery Row and the Salvador Dali museum.

As we approached Paso Robles on our return, Manny and I were both feeling jittery, but once inside the vintner's house, there was nothing much to it. We followed his instructions to a t, transferring the wine from tank to oak cask, and then hauling the cask to the trunk of the car. We vowed to drink it in a year's time.

Driving through Big Sur some hours later, the sea shining like cellophane through the evergreens, Manny quoted Kerouac out of the blue: "the only people for me are the mad ones, the ones who are mad to live, mad to talk, mad to be saved…'"

"Didn't Kerouac basically die of wine?" I asked.

"Yeah," Manny replied. "But first he lived of it."

We didn't talk much for the rest of the drive. I can't speak for Manny, but I was thinking of Queen Califia and her griffins. I believed in them.

A year later, to the day, I was back in California, pouring the wine. Manny and I raised a toast to the vintner and his family, and to our own ongoing friendship. After our first sip, we praised the wine to the sky, but by the third glass--*in vino veritas*--our inhibitions were gone. The truth is, it was just okay. I don't know, maybe we had done something wrong, but you can get a Pinot noir every bit as heady for like fifteen bucks at Costco.

*Tom Gammarino is author of the novels King of the Worlds (Chin Music Press, 2016) and Big in Japan (Chin Music Press, 2009), and the novella Jellyfish Dreams (Amazon Kindle Single, 2012). Shorter works have appeared in American Short Fiction, The Writer, Entropy, The New York Review of Science Fiction, The Tahoma Literary Review, The New York Tyrant, Bamboo Ridge, Hawai'i Pacific Review, and The Hawai'i Review, among others. He holds an MFA in Creative Writing from The New School and a PhD in English from the University of Hawai'i, and has received a Fulbright fellowship in creative writing and the Elliot Cades Award for Literature, Hawai'i's highest literary honor.*

# MR. DESSY

## *by Brian Lillie*

C arla hadn't been to the Thursday night St. Ambrose meeting in more than a year and didn't recognize anybody besides Nellie S.; otherwise, it was all men—three twitchy types who smelled of B.O. and looked like they hadn't eaten in days, one silent old-timer in a corduroy jacket, others. Her teeth felt too big for her mouth. It was hard for her not to stare at the shadows in the corners of the room. They looked alarmingly wet, as if freshly smeared onto the cinderblock walls.

When it was her turn to speak, Carla tried to concentrate on her breathing, but her mind broke off in several directions, flowing with chatter, no idea what her mouth was saying, hoping to hell she wasn't acting crazy on this night of all nights.

*Act normal. Act normal. Act normal.*

Then it was over. In the past, Nellie would ask the attendees to hold hands at the end of meetings during the Lord's Prayer, but thankfully she didn't this time, possibly because everyone looked so contagious.

On 'Amen', Carla jumped right up and started stacking chairs, forcefully ignoring the men and their hungry souls, refusing to look at the wet shadows. By the time she returned to drag the second stack into the janitor's closet, the meth brigade was gone, leaving all their half-drunk coffee cups and other trash strewn about.

Nellie shook her head, jingling her huge earrings. "A bunch of little piggies," she said. "How've you been, Miss Carla?"

"I'm... okay," Carla mumbled.

Nellie nodded. "Are you still at the shelter?"

"No. A few of us have a place now. On Needham Hill."

"Well, that's great news, honey! It does my old heart good to see folks really turning their lives around."

"Yes." Carla forced herself not to think of William.

*Act normal.*

"How now, mad spirit?" A thin line of spit stretched between the one-eared man's lips when he spoke. His eyes were two pinpricks of intensity wriggling on his scarred face like a pair of insects. "Hast thou the flower there?" he said.

Carla slipped off her backpack. She had crouched behind a graffiti covered transformer box up on the road for more than an hour, talking herself into climbing down here into the near dark below the overpass. She hadn't seen anyone else but was losing control of her breathing nonetheless. It felt like countless men with dirty hands were watching her from the shadows. Memories were clawing up from her guts. The occasional rumble of cars overhead punctuated her growing panic.

The one-eared man smiled as she unzipped the backpack. "I pray thee, give it me," he whispered, edging closer.

Carla was afraid if she opened her mouth she would start screaming and wouldn't be able to stop, so she just reached into the pack and pulled out the bag. She held it out to the man, not daring to step toward him. The one-eared man surprised her by standing up from his crouch, brushing off his filthy jacket, and gingerly taking the bag from her. His eyes wiggled crazily when he opened it and peered inside.

Carla flashed on that horrible night when she was ten. The shadows had poured from the sky in every direction as she ran away from the funeral home. All she could see was Grandma Ruth's empty, putty-soft face lying in the open casket, a doorway to endless darkness. When her caseworker, Mr. Charles, finally found her hours later she had been huddled down here beneath the overpass, nearly catatonic with terror.

"Oft have I heard that grief softens the mind and makes it fearful and degenerate," said the one-eared man, not looking up. "Think therefore on revenge and cease to weep."

"That's what you asked for," said Carla, tilting her chin toward the paper bag, though it felt like someone else was speaking. "You said you'd tell me about Mr. Dessy."

The man looked up at her, as if just noticing she was there. "Did we fuck?"

"No!" Carla's voice reverberated against the cracked concrete like a gunshot.

Carla helped Nellie put away the literature and clean the coffee maker in the grubby little kitchen area.

"Well," she said too loudly while drying her hands. "I have a bus to catch."

Nellie flashed her another thousand-watt smile. "It was a real treat, Miss Carla. You take care now. And maybe come back again sometime soon, okay?"

Carla didn't know what to say to that, so she just nodded some more and headed out of the Community Room toward the front door. Once in the outer hallway, she leaned against a wall and took a deep breath to calm her fizzing nerves. Listening to make sure Nellie wasn't following, she quickly slipped off her boots. With a deep breath and one big mental push she ran to the front door, opened it loudly onto the drizzly night, and then tiptoed down the dark hall in her stocking feet. By the time the door clanked shut she was hidden behind the trophy case near Father Buchanan's office.

Nellie left ten minutes later, talking loudly on her cellphone as she locked up. Carla watched through one of the windows until Nellie and her multicolored umbrella blurred in the rainy darkness and disappeared.

William showed up at the apartment, clean-shaven, three weeks after Carla, Old Nancy, and Rose moved in. He brought a bucket of Kentucky Fried Chicken and a 2-liter bottle of Red Pop and smiled like a preacher when Rose met him at the front door. Carla and Old Nancy hung back, watching from the dining room table, where just a moment before the three of them had been sorting coupons. William touched Rose's bare arm. She giggled. Old Nancy exhaled a cloud of blue smoke, muttering something under her breath.

The food was welcome, in any case, and soon everyone was chowing down. It had been awhile since Carla had eaten any meat and the chicken tasted really good.

"This was *so* thoughtful of you," Rose said, gesturing at the various tubs of coleslaw and potatoes perspiring on the table.

"I just thought you ladies might be able to use a good meal is all," said William.

Later, Old Nancy locked herself in her room while Rose and William tangled on the couch, pretending to watch *Real Housewives of Santa Barbara* with the volume turned up way too high. Carla could feel a change in the air, as if something rancid had floated into the apartment. She vomited in the bathroom and snuck out, wandering the streets until sunrise with the greasy ghost of fried chicken haunting her mouth.

Rose met her at the door when she got home, looking radiantly mussed in her old yellow nightgown. "William just got back to town. He's going to be staying with us for a couple weeks, okay?" she asked.

Carla's stomach lurched. A stab of red flashed in her vision, surprising in its jealous intensity. Rose had obviously been up for hours practicing that question and Carla knew that if she opened her mouth she'd say something crazy that would make Rose cry. So she just nodded and forced a smile and did her best to ignore the shadows thickening in the corners of the living room as she skulked off to her bed.

Carla walked all the hallways on all three floors of the school twice, entered every bathroom, swept her flashlight around every empty class-room. None of it rang a bell in her foggy memory.

Just as she was beginning to despair, a sudden memory seized her. She ran to the moonlit gymnasium, burst through the doors, her footsteps reverberating. She rushed to the old bleachers, praying they hadn't been replaced since her senior year. She climbed behind them and scanned the bottoms of the topmost bleachers with her flashlight. Nothing. She climbed farther underneath.

There they were.

Though they'd been painted over, maybe several times, the symbols were still visible if you knew what you were looking for, cut into the under-side of one of the middle bleacher benches. She could almost feel Roger Temple hunched down, squinting as he scratched the symbols into the wood with his pocketknife, not knowing he had less than a year to go. That he'd be 16 forever.

She copied it all down in her notebook and got the fuck out of there.

It had been easy enough to get blood from Rose. Old Nancy was well past menopause, so Carla only needed to wait until a used tampon appeared in the bathroom trash. Likewise, as far as gathering some of Rose's hair, which grew down almost to her ass—it was a simple matter of checking the shower drain, especially since Old Nancy was basically bald under her wigs, and Carla herself still only showered at the Y.

Getting hold of the same from William proved much trickier. There was never a time when Carla was alone with him in the apartment during the day; his lieutenant, Dooley, was always lounging on the couch. Or one of their 'customers' would be standing sheepishly in the kitchen, filthy bills clutched in their filthier hands.

"Either stay in your room or get the fuck out of here, freak," William would say if Carla lingered in the living room for more than a minute. "You look like a goddamn narc."

In Group, Dr. Allison would sometimes ring a bell whenever anyone used what she called "magical thinking". It was one of those little round ones with a button on top, like from a movie where the snooty concierge rings for the goofy bellboy.

Roger Temple showed up one week, tiny and pale, plunked down between Jill and Preston in the spot Oliver had occupied just the week before. "Guys, please welcome our newest member, Roger," Dr. Allison had said in that unconscious radio announcer voice she used around new people.

Carla hadn't run into anyone else from school at the hospital in the seven months she'd been going to Group, and had been happy about that. Initially, she thought everyone at St. Ambrose hated her. Ding!

"Why do you think that, Carla?"

"Because they laugh when I turn my back." Ding!

"Can you hear them laugh?"

"It's more like they make faces." Ding!

"Roger, you're in Carla's class: do you notice your classmates making faces and laughing behind Carla's back?"

The energy in the apartment often felt like a burning beehive. On those nights, Carla would have to flee from the snickering idiots in the living room to go sleep in the shelter or on one of the benches in the courtyard outside the law school on Edison Avenue. She would lie there, planning to leave the apartment for good, maybe even skip town completely, but then she'd inevitably see Rose in her mind's eye, floating like a speck in a sea of Nothing, which would stir the shadows in her guts. Carla would have to bite down hard on whatever she had at hand—her coat, a stick, her arm—to get them to quiet back down.

One night, Carla snuck into the apartment late, hoping to avoid William, or anyone really. He was sprawled out on the couch with a bottle, watching basketball, and sneered as she entered. Threat congealed like bacon fat in the dark corners of the living room.

"Little Miss Sunshine is back," he said, raising his bottle in mock toast. "You must be exhausted from your day of doing whatever the fuck you do. Come on over and watch the game with me."

She tried to ignore him, took a few steps toward the bedroom hallway.

"Seriously, get over here."

"No thank you," Carla murmured. Almost to the hallway, she could see the door to her room. Her legs were shaking so badly, she thought they might crack apart.

William was behind her suddenly, sour gin breath leaking down her neck. He grabbed her wrist and swung her around, eyes reddish black, deadly. "It's not really a request, is it?" he said, dragging her easily to the couch and forcing her to sit.

The television was a faraway jumble of colors and sound. Carla's mind couldn't hold onto any of it. The room was shrinking, dimming.

William stared at her for several long seconds, unblinking. Finally, he grinned. "I had to smack Rose around a little today," he said.

Carla's brain went completely still.

"She wanted me to move out—can you believe that bitch? After all I've been doing for you girls." William giggled and patted Carla on the thigh. "Don't you worry, though. She's fine. Just a little lover's quarrel. And you'll be happy to know I'm staying."

One night in late spring, Carla stayed at the shelter, to nurse her fraying mind and maybe go to the 8 p.m. meeting there. While waiting in line to sign in for the night, she saw an old acquaintance from high school walk by on the street, laughing with a tall man in sandals. Sylvia Matthews. They didn't wave or make eye contact or anything, but just seeing her jolted Carla and, like a black egg cracking open in her mind, reminded her of Roger Temple, the fire at his uncle's house, and Mr. Dessy.

The following morning she had gone in search of the one-eared man.

Carla's luck changed on a Tuesday night when she came back to the apartment after having been gone for two days. The place was a shambles. Rose was cooing over William on the couch, dabbing with a wet washcloth at the blood starting to coagulate on the side of his face. Rose looked up and smiled sadly.

"Everything okay?" said Carla.

"Not for that little fuck, Dooley," said William, fuming.

"There was a fight," said Rose. Her eyes looked old and exhausted.

"No shit, there was a fight. She can see that, dumbass."

Rose bit back a response and dabbed some more at the gash on William's head. Carla edged closer. "You're gonna need stitches," she said.

"Fuck that," said William.

"I can do 'em for you," said Carla, meeting his gaze, trying not to get sucked into the vortex of his anger.

"Seriously?"

Carla nodded. "Unless you're too much of a pussy." She felt the floor lurch beneath her. Her vision flickered. She'd gone too far with that comment.

*Shut up. Shut up. Shut up.*

William laughed, thank God. "All right, bitch. Go get your sewing kit," he said, slapping Rose's hand away. "I wanna look good for when I go cut that motherfucker's balls off."

Carla took the #12 bus all the way out to the edge of town, getting off in the dust near the county dump as evening began its slow, late summer descent. She hiked down the road, cut through the abandoned drive-in, and slipped through a tear in the weedy fence behind where the screen used to stand. It took awhile, but she eventually found the path through the woods and followed it down to the tattered banks of Mosquito Lake as night finally fell.

Carla went down to the water's edge, where she emptied most of a can of Deep Woods Off onto herself. Her face tingled and her eyes stung until she blinked them to tears.

With light from the flashlight set atop her backpack in the wet dirt, she began drawing the symbols on the shore with a stick, as close to the water as she could.

Once that was done she pulled out the plastic grocery bag from her pack. She opened the can of sterno and placed it in the center of the middle symbol, per the one-eared man's instructions, lighting it with the candle lighter she'd shoplifted from the grocery store that morning.

Carla looked out at the water, glinting dully in the waxing moonlight. Frogs and crickets had joined the buzzing chorus of the mosquitos. A small splash sounded as a fish crested somewhere in the darkness.

It was time.

While concentrating on Rose's sad face in her mind's eye, Carla dropped the used tampon and small tangle of Rose's hair into the flame, where it shriveled and sparked, giving off a horrid stench. Next, she forced herself to picture William, while adding the bloody gauze and the few strands of his hair she'd managed to save from stitching him up the night before.

Carla pricked her finger with the corner of a razor blade and squeezed three drops of blood into the fire. Wincing, she plucked a few hairs from her head and watched them dwindle to nothing in the flames.

When she was satisfied the offerings had fully burnt, Carla stood and faced the lake.

*Mr. Dessy hear my prayer*
*Sleeping in your midnight lair*
*Take these gifts of blood and fire*
*Give to me my heart's desire.*
*Mr. Dessy fast asleep*
*I call to you in your chambers deep*
*Like a storm upon the lake*
*I beg of you, my vengeance take.*

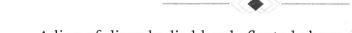

A line of disembodied heads floated above dark water in a starless sky. They were all different ages and races, men and women, stretching into the distance like a bizarre necklace. The only face she recognized was Roger Temple's, which was at the front of the line. His eyes were open wide, staring right at her.

"He had to burn," said Roger Temple.

"I know," said Carla.

There was a loud splash.

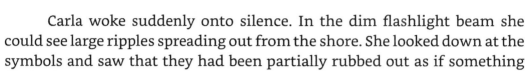

Carla woke suddenly onto silence. In the dim flashlight beam she could see large ripples spreading out from the shore. She looked down at the symbols and saw that they had been partially rubbed out as if something big had been dragged across them. The sterno can was gone.

The depth of the quiet hit her all at once—no frogs, no crickets, no mosquitos—and she nearly screamed in utter terror. Or maybe she *did* scream. Then she found herself running through dark trees, away from the lake, mind swirling, blackness threatening to swallow her up—

Rose spent the morning getting ready for their two week visit, rushing around the apartment with a rag, wiping away non-existent dust and cobwebs, arranging and then rearranging the meager furniture and the five books on the lone shelf in the living room.

"If you two aren't going to help," she clucked at Old Nancy and Carla. "At least get out of my way."

Old Nancy shook her head and chuckled. "Where's the fire? We ain't hosting the Queen Mother."

Rose stopped in mid flurry and put her thin arms on her hips. Carla almost laughed at Rose's attempt at a stern face, but assumed that wouldn't be appreciated in the moment. "You two—geesh. And don't even *think* about smoking in here today."

"That reminds me," said Old Nancy, who saluted and headed to her room.

"She better not be smoking in there," Rose said.

Their case worker, LaTonya, met them at the apartment at 5:30 on the dot. After looking around and politely declining Rose's offer of coffee, she got down to business. "So far, so good, ladies. I'm impressed with how the transition is going. I do think you could be buying more fresh fruits and veggies, of course, but overall you three are on my 'nice' list."

Carla watched Rose's smile as LaTonya spoke. She actually seemed to grow larger when she smiled. It was a beautiful sight and it made Carla feel uncomfortably warm.

"So, the last thing we need to go over is the drug testing schedule.

The State has randomized that process now, so there's no advance warning anymore. You can assume that one of you will be up for testing every 90 days, though, for the first year. If all goes well, that will reduce to every six months in year two. Remember, there's now a Zero Tolerance policy. One strike from any of you, or any houseguests, and you're all evicted. Any questions?"

The night lasts a year, a lifetime.

Everywhere is darkness.

Shadows breed unchecked like larvae, crawling and festering, unseen.

She must keep moving.

Blood trickles from the top of her head. Did she hit it on something? *You're gonna need stitches.*

She can't stop running. She must keep moving.

If she stops, the shadows in her guts will take full form and drag her away. Ding!

*How do you know they'll drag you away?*

Because they told me. Ding! Ding! Ding!

She unspools.

Carla always thought of Roger Temple as 'Roger Temple', never just Roger. This was because the word 'Temple' always felt so soothing and light to her. And since 'Roger' meant 'yes' or 'okay' in all those war movies she used to watch with Grandma Ruth, 'Roger Temple' was like a double rainbow of a word. She would sometimes say his name quietly to herself as she walked home from St. Ambrose. But not in a romantic way, she was pretty sure.

These were the kinds of things she could never tell Dr. Allison, who was like a coach or something, always vaguely shallow even when trying to be deep. Carla knew Dr. A. would not be able to deal with the size and weight of words, or how Carla's teeth sometimes felt like they were separate from her body like little insects living in her mouth.

Carla's dreams were often filled with the sound of Roger Temple sobbing, as he did most weeks in Group. Sometimes she would awaken from these dreams with tears streaming down her cheeks. She knew he was close to shattering.

Somehow it was daylight. Sunrise trickled slowly over the horizon, dragging color back to the stubborn grey city. Carla had lost her boots somewhere in the night and her bare feet were filthy, the left one bleeding. She was covered in bruises, scratches, mosquito bites. The few people she passed on the sidewalk gave her a wide berth.

At the YMCA, she spent a good 20 minutes in the shower, not caring when the hot water ran out.

All she wanted to do was sleep, but she couldn't go back to the apartment and the shelter wouldn't be open for another several hours. In the end, she tried her luck in the stacks of the undergraduate library by the arboretum and managed to get in a couple hours of deathly blackness before security rousted her.

She was back on the pavement, limping along on increasingly sore feet, when the sky began to turn an angry green. Carla felt strangely giddy, happy even. Somehow the oncoming storm increased this feeling of well-being, and as the temperature dropped and the wind picked up, she laughed out loud.

Something was most definitely about to happen.

They crouched down low to avoid being seen up on the roof of the school, though it was so late the chances of being caught were slim. The late October night had taken a sudden turn toward the oncoming winter. In the shadowed orange glow from the streetlights below, Roger Temple looked almost skeletal, skinny arms wrapped around skinny knees for warmth.

"This is going to sound nuts," he said after a long shared silence. "Like, really, *really* nuts. You have to promise me you won't say anything to Dr. A. about this, and I *mean* it. She'd definitely help my parents send me away, if she knew."

"I won't say anything. I never talk to anybody."

"That's true. Okay. It's like... I think I found somebody who can help me with my problem."

"A new therapist?"

Roger Temple laughed. "No! I found somebody who has *real* powers. He helps people who have nowhere else to turn. The thing is... they say if you want to meet him, you gotta talk to his agent, and the only way to find his agent, is to go to the scariest place you can think of." He looked right into Carla's eyes.

She had been focusing on his voice instead of the thickening shadows that surrounded them, and wasn't sure if she should speak. "Where's the scariest place?" she asked, finally.

"See, that's the thing. It all sounds so fucking nuts, but I went there last night, to my Uncle Phil's house. He's in a play downtown, so I knew he wouldn't be there. I broke into his basement. I could barely force myself to go in, I was shaking so bad. What if Uncle Phil came home early and heard me? What if he found me down there. What if..." Roger Temple closed his eyes for a long moment, and when he opened them again they looked like the bottoms of two black wells. "The fucking one-eared man was waiting for me down there, Carla. Just like they said."

"Who?"

Roger smiled. "He told me Mr. Dessy would be happy to help."

William woke with a start.

He rubbed at the inflamed stitches on his cheek, moaning quietly. The storm still raged outside.

Lightning flashed.

Mr. Dessy smiled.

"Jesus Christ!" yelled William, barely audible above the crescendo of thunder that shook the room. He kicked out wildly. Mr. Dessy reared up on his hind legs and crashed down on William's chest, pinning him to the couch with a loud crunch of cracking ribs.

William beat at Mr. Dessy's shell with his fists, like punching a wet boulder, tried to wriggle out from under the creature's grinding bulk.

Carla reached over from her spot against the wall and flipped on the overhead light. William's crazed eyes met her gaze, surprised. "I'm gonna cut your fucking tits off," he gasped.

Carla stepped closer. "It's time for you to go," she whispered.

"Fuck you, freak." William turned to Mr. Dessy. "And fuck you, too," he said, even as his eyes went wide with renewed terror.

Mr. Dessy stretched out his neck until his beaked face was barely an inch from William's. The creature's breath was like muck and dead fish and smoke and it filled the room. His voice was worse.

*DOWN DOWN DOWN, INTO THE OOZE YOU GO*

Mr. Dessy chuckled and bit off William's left ear. Blood poured down the side of the couch as William shrieked and flailed around.

*DOWN DOWN DOWN*

Carla almost vomited, but forced herself to keep watching. Mr. Dessy was somehow both real and not real at the same time, like a churning whirlpool of mud forced into a shape. One moment he was the dark outline of a large man, and the next a spike-covered nightmare turtle-thing. In that moment, His true name came to Carla, ancient and heavy, but she refused to think it. Just the slightest taste of the word felt like a long tunnel into endless cold murk, and she recoiled.

Instead, she leaned in to William, who was mostly quiet now, even as the blood spurted from his head and the creature loomed over him with black reptilian eyes. "I'll tell Rose you said goodbye."

Mr. Dessy whispered into William's remaining ear until he stopped breathing.

Carla was on the road as the sun came up. She had walked a good portion of the night and was mostly dry by then, though she shivered even as the air began to warm around her.

The one-eared man was waiting for her at the abandoned drive in, sitting cross-legged in the wet dirt by the collapsed refreshment stand. Carla was too exhausted to say anything to him, or to even gesture. He got up and followed her through the rip in the back fence, matching her gait with his hands in his pockets.

The lake was quiet and smooth, with wisps of fog still clinging to the edges and mingling in the reeds. The one-eared man stood at the waterside and peered out. In the clear morning light, Carla could see that the entire back of his head was an uneven quilt of burn scarring.

"I hold the world but as the world, Gratiano; A stage where every man must play a part, and mine is a sad one," he said, without turning to look at her.

Carla didn't know how to respond. Instead, she dropped to her knees and clasped her hands in front of her. "Thank you, Mr. Dessy, for fulfilling my heart's desire," she whispered.

The one-eared man called out in some language she didn't recognize. He stepped into the lake, causing no ripples. Carla watched until the water was up to his neck, and then turned away. When she looked again a moment later, it was like he had never existed in the first place.

Carla passed William on her way back up the path from the lake. He stumbled along, going in the opposite direction. He wore a cheap black funeral suit, and his glazed eyes didn't seem to notice her at all, even when they walked right by each other. Where his left ear had been was now an angry, oozing scab. She was glad to not have to say anything to him.

On her way out of town, Carla stopped briefly at a boarded up gas station by the old fairgrounds and managed to force the backdoor partially open so she could squeeze inside. Per the final instruction, she scratched the symbols into the dust-furred wooden front counter using her key from the apartment. She could almost feel the symbols on the bleacher at St. Ambrose disappear as she carved, and with them her final proof that Roger Temple had ever lived.

Carla shoved her way back outside and stood for a moment on the weed-cracked asphalt, scanning the empty horizon as the afternoon sun brightened like a furnace.

She hoped Rose wouldn't be too mad at her for leaving.

After a few deep breaths, Carla set off to the West, with no destination in mind.

Love was such a complicated thing.

*Brian Lillie is a writer and musician from Ann Arbor, Michigan, USA. He has had a few stories published in recent years, most notably in NEW FEARS I (Titan Books, edited by Mark Morris), Albedo One issue 48, and SINGLE SLICES (Cutting Block Books, edited by Patrick Beltran). He releases albums under the name Lionbelly and is currently at work on his first novel.*

# KATU LATU KULU

*By Gregory J. Wolos*

**M**ira and I look down at the sandwich bag on our kitchen table. It came inside the business letter-sized envelope sent us without a return address. Mira blows inside the empty envelope to puff it open wider, stares inside, turns it over and shakes it again like she's salting soup before setting it down. She gives me a look through her thick glasses that might be bemusement, might be suspicion, might go as far as accusation.

"No note this time either," she says. Her gaze drops to the sealed baggie, which I hold up to the lamp suspended over the table. I flick my wrist, and the spoonful of gray dust settles into a corner of the bag.

"Why do you keep touching it?" Mira asks. "How do we know it isn't poisonous? Maybe its laced with whatever the Russians use. Some kind of nerve thing. A poison that strong might get through the plastic."

I don't put down the bag just yet, though I'm not looking at the powder any longer—I'm looking through the plastic and on through the picture window that faces the stretch of green lawn I've paid somebody to mow for years. Mowing had been my son Jesse's job during his teens. For the biggest expanse, he abandoned the neat back-and-forth rows I'd instructed him to make. Instead, he mowed in a counter-clockwise, squared-off spiral that wound up in the center of the yard. "It's all half turns to the left," he explained. "Ninety degrees. Saves time. Your way, you have to make a complete about-face each row—180 degrees. Wastes time." Frankly, Jesse's spiral reminded me of those alien crop patterns you read about. But I let him do it his way—it showed ingenuity, and he was the one doing the work. Now that he's gone, I miss the spirals. Right now, the river reflects the sky with the quivering luminescence of a dying fluorescent bulb.

"This one's the same as all the others," I tell Mira, and lay the bag down on the envelope. "If they were poisonous to touch, we'd be dead by now." This is our fifth bag. Bags two, three, and four are in the shoebox that's also on the table between my wife and me. The first bag we dismissed as a joke or mistaken delivery; only after the second envelope showed up a week later did we get curious.

"Not if the poison's slow-acting," Mira says. She takes off her glasses and rubs her eyes. When she takes her hand away, her unmagnified eyes are as tiny as a mole's.

"What if I sniff it?" I tease, lifting the bag under my nose.

"Don't you dare!" Mira puts her glasses back on, and her gray irises fill the frames like worn silver dollars.

"Maybe it's just a spice," I say. "It looks a little like ground pepper. Maybe somebody gave us a subscription to 'Spice of the Week' as a surprise."

"But why would they keep sending us the same thing over and over?"

"Maybe they're just lousy at their job. Or—" and I bend over the baggie, nearly resting my chin on the table, "—maybe there are subtle differences only a finely trained spice-ologist would notice." I sit back in my chair, struck by a new thought. "What about gunpowder? Does it look like this?"

Mira blinks. The rims of her lids are bright red. When did she lose her eyelashes? Does she see anything missing when she looks at me? "I don't know. Does it?" she asks.

I shake my head. "Who do I look like, Alfred Nobel?"

"Who—?"

"Alfred Nobel. He invented dynamite. He felt guilty that he got rich making something so destructive, so he came up with the Nobel prizes. There must be places where we could have this stuff analyzed. Is it time for us to call the authorities?"

Mira pulls the lapels of her flower print robe together at the throat. "What if it's an illegal substance and we get in trouble?"

"But we didn't do anything."

"Maybe we became responsible once we accepted that first bag. 'Possession is nine-tenths of the law.'"

I label bag number five with an indelible marker, date it, and stick it in the shoebox. "Should we keep the shoebox in the freezer? Maybe whatever-it-is will keep longer. Like the first fish I caught when we moved here —that big bottom feeder I pulled out of the river. Remember how I'd take it out of the freezer to show people? 'Poor man's taxidermy,' I called it."

Mira rolls her eyes, and her pupils swim in unison around her irises. "I don't want poison in the refrigerator," she says. "Put it all back in the basement. It's cool enough down there. But not too close to the furnace—just in case it's flammable."

"Explosive?" I try to think of an Alfred Nobel quip, but come up empty.

"Who's to say?"

Bag number six, containing another scoop of the mystery substance, shows up nine days later. Same size envelope, again without a return address. Mira wants me to handle the envelopes and bags with latex gloves. As I tug a pair on, I feel like I'm preparing to read something like the Guttenberg Bible in the rare books room of some important library. But the gloves are uncomfortable—my skin inside them feels like its suffocating. After a minute I peel the gloves off and my pale hands emerge, looking like the flesh of some exotic fruit.

What about the postmark, you're probably asking. The truth is, none are the same.

"I'm going to start charting postmarks on a map to see if there's a pattern," I tell Mira.

"There *is* a pattern," she says. "They're all sent from places we've never been."

"Seems pretty random," I say. I pinch the grit collected in the corner of the newest baggie. "It's hard to believe all of this is being arranged just for us." My fingernails are too long. I showed Jesse how to trim his when he was little—he got one set of fingers done but couldn't manipulate the clippers with his off hand, and I had to finish for him. I don't know when he learned to complete the job on his own.

I have an inspiration: "Have we got any magnets anywhere? Maybe these are iron filings." I picture a dirty hand with a file, sawing away at the bars of a prison—from inside or outside—escape or rescue?

"Check the refrigerator," Mira says.

"We keep magnets in the refrigerator?"

"Not *in*—*on*. The alphabet letters."

I look into the kitchen at the refrigerator. On its door are a half dozen magnet-backed letters, Jesse's when he was a pre-schooler. Mira fished them out of storage two years ago, and since then they've sunk below knee level, down so low you'd think they'd be easy to ignore. This is the first time we've mentioned them since the tragedy. The *S* and the *A* are lowest, either winning the race to the floor or losing the battle against gravity, followed by the *T*. The *H* and *O* lag. Though they're scrambled, these are the letters that would spell the name of our promised grandson, Thomas. The letters—red, blue, two yellows, and a green—were resurrected when we learned our son's wife Anna was pregnant with a boy they'd already named. Petite Anna — I picture her standing in front of the fridge, frowning, her small hands settled on her swollen belly that was only inches from the letters she bowed over.

"Are these letters clean?" she asked with a sweet fastidiousness we connected to her approaching motherhood.

"I soaked them in bleach," Mira said, "and then I ran them through the dishwasher. They couldn't be cleaner."

The girl's eyes lit up (she was nearly thirty, no longer a girl, really) and her lips parted as she reached toward the spelled-out name as if it were the baby itself. Then with busy fingers she rearranged the letters, arching her neck to see over her belly.

"'S-M-O-T-H-A.' What's '*SMOTHA*' mean?" She grinned at the three of us watching her—her husband and her in-laws, seated around the same table on which the shoe box of mysterious baggies now lies.

*SMOTHA.* Sounds like "some other." Sounds like "his mother." Sounds like "smother."

Thoughts never articulated, never shared, but as stark as the letters spelling HOLLYWOOD across the shaggy hills slouching toward the Pacific coast. Only in a nightmare would we have anticipated a mother's fatal hemorrhaging, a would-have-been-orphaned infant choked umbilically during his failed birth. No longer a husband, never a father, our despondent son chose his own strangulation in a sealed garage with a running engine. *SMOTHA.*

I linger in front of the refrigerator, wondering which magnetic letter to choose to test the dust in my baggies. Which of my feelings overlap with those of the daughter-in-law who'd stood in exactly this spot three lifetimes ago? I pick the red *O* magnet, biting my lip over the ironies of my choice: circle of life? bloody opening? Zero satisfaction. Returning to the kitchen table—Mira has left—I stare through the center of the *O* as if I'm frying an ant with a magnifying glass, then swipe the magnetic letter over the newest baggie. I wait like an angler for the faintest tug. Nothing. I shake the contents, flip the bag, try again. Not a single particle is attracted to my red *O*. I run the magnet over the rest of the bags with the same result. Whatever the substance Mira and I are receiving, it's not iron. Unless I'm using a dud magnet. But if it were a dud, the letter couldn't have clung to the refrigerator for so long.

Why, you're probably wondering, haven't we considered ashes? It's what the dust most resembles—crushed, burnt out embers. I'd say our hesitance over accepting the ashes as ashes is like searching for lost keys: don't you put off checking the most likely hiding place? Because if the keys aren't there, where else is there to look? Admitting right off that the substance in our baggies is ashes might feel too much like a trip to the dark side of the moon.

Three more baggies are delivered over the next month. Mira and I now acknowledge that the gray spoonful of matter in each bag is ashes. The last envelope is identical to all the others, except it has an airmail stamp. It's postmarked "Biarritz, France." We look it up and discover that Biarritz is a resort town on the Atlantic coast a few miles from the border of Spain. Basque country.

"I thought Biarritz was in Switzerland," Mira says.

"I would have guessed Belgium."

The *O* magnet is back on the refrigerator. I debated between placing it immediately before or after the *H*. "*OH*" or "*HO*? "*OH*" indicates surprise. "*HO*" is snarky. On a whim, I stick the *O* after the *M*. "*MO*"—who doesn't want more? I wouldn't put it past Mira to move the *O* in front of the *M*. *OM* —that mystical syllable you hear Buddhist's chant. Both "*MO*" and "*OM*" are incomplete "*MOM*"s.

Maybe it's the nearly-but-not quite *MOM* that leads to my dream of Anna. Anna appears there as a shimmery new acquaintance. She describes an incident she says she witnessed while serving in the Peace Corps in Madagascar. In the remotest forests of that island nation's villages, she explains, vanilla farmers defend their crops from poachers with machetes. The seed-filled pods—which, when crushed, might resemble the baggie dust— fetch nearly the same price as the equivalent weight in silver. The actual Anna preferred a natural look, but this is, after all, a dream, and Dream-Anna wears bright red lipstick and purple eye shadow. Her cheeks are heavily rouged. She dons eyeglasses that look just like Mira's, and for just a second my daughter-in-law's shadowed eyelids flutter like twin purple moths. Then the lenses turn into mirrors for a moment, reflecting duplicate faces I recognize as my own. Dream-Anna removes the glasses.

"Biarritz." She exhales with a sigh that carries the scent of vanilla. "Jesse and I had planned to take our honeymoon there. We thought maybe we'd see the green ray over the sea when the sun set. There's a French movie about the green ray. Do you know about it? Some call it a 'flash.' It comes and goes in the blink of an eye—a burst of green, just as the sun disappears below the horizon. But the conditions need to be perfect. No clouds or haze. Sightings are rare." The vanilla odor is overpowering. I recall deep licks from an ice cream cone—the flavor rolls over my tongue like it did when I was a child. Now I'm looking at what I know are Madagascar farmers closing in a circle, machetes raised. They hack soundlessly at something in the center of their ring.

"The penalty for vanilla theft is death," Anna's disembodied voice informs. "The community enforces the punishment."

"What happens if you see the green flash?" I ask, trying to not lose hold of at least one thread.

"Your heart opens to whoever you're with," Dream-Anna says. "And their heart opens to you."

The next morning at breakfast I ask Mira if she remembers a movie about a green flash that opens lovers' hearts to each other. "I think it's set in Biarritz. Did Jesse and Anna ever plan to take their honeymoon there?"

Mira frowns. "They never talked about anywhere but Barbados," she says. "And they loved it there, in spite of the rain. I've heard of the green ray, though, but not from a movie. There's a book with that name. By Jules Verne? I read it when I was a kid. I forgot the part about knowing what's in your lover's heart." She takes a bite from her cinnamon raisin toast, chews thoughtfully. "You must have Biarritz on your mind because of yesterday's letter."

"And Anna served in the Peace Corps in the Ukraine, right? She told us a story about how the woman whose house she stayed at buttered her shoes once without asking. To make them shiny."

"Yes, the Ukraine. A little village where she was giving English lessons to children in an orphanage. Then the Russians invaded, and the Peace Corps gave her the choice of transferring to a different location or quitting and coming back to America. I think maybe they offered her Madagascar."

I feel the blood moving in my cheeks, but is it rushing in or draining out? "Madagascar, of course. Why didn't I remember that?"

"Because she didn't go," Mira says. "She came home. And after that she met Jesse in graduate school."

We've been getting these bags for a year, but we've gained no information about the smatterings of dust that keep arriving. I feel like a frog in a heating pot of water—what won't I tolerate before I'm boiled? Are we at the center of some invisible web or dangling from an outer strand? The spider or its victim? The Sun or Pluto? The envelopes pile up, but Mira and I have yet to share the details of our situation with anyone outside of our home.

"Maybe there's something else we should be doing," Mira says this morning. "Do you think there's an implied task we're missing—maybe we were supposed to get instructions with the first envelope. Like a chain letter. I've been looking into them. Could it be we're intended to send these bags back out—or new bags of our own? Maybe a good luck chain—there's a Hawaiian one where you send a pictograph to ten people. Or the famous 'Katu Latu Kulu' chain—the threat is that if you don't continue it, a murdered princess will show up in your bedroom on the night of a full moon and steal your soul."

Mira clasps her hands. She rubs her wedding band with her thumb, and I peer down at my own ring. I haven't taken it off in decades—my knuckle has swollen too much. If I ever wanted the ring removed, I'd have to have it sawed off. But look how thin the skin is on the back of our hands— wrinkled as crepe paper—barely enough flesh to cover our bones.

"I did my own research," I say. "About getting the ashes tested. Online it says that the cremation process destroys DNA, except for maybe fragments of bones and teeth, and those are usually pulverized into powder and get so mixed up with everything else that they don't leave a traceable genetic footprint. So there's only a slim chance that we'd be able to find out whose ashes we keep getting."

Mira's head snaps back as if she's just broken an ammonia capsule under her nose. "When did we agree that they were *human* ashes? Couldn't they just be from fireplace logs or cigarette butts? Cremated mice even?" She retreats to her chain letter idea. "Do we resend the ashes we've got or get some of our own from somewhere—fresh ashes. Whatever kind of ashes they are, how do we decide who to send them to?"

I think of Jesse. And of Anna and Thomas. Mira must wonder, as I do, if the ash-baggies are somehow connected to them. So much stopped when we lost the kids. Whether we're on the edge of things or in the middle, we're stuck in a continuous present—memories are too painful, and there's no future to speak of. But are the two of us even living in the same present? Mira is obsessed with her "chain" theories, while I keep nodding toward DNA sampling, in spite of the doubtful return. Are both of us pretending curiosity to disguise the fact that we're only treading water?

"I thought maybe I'd send some ashes to one of those ancestry places anyway on the off chance something comes up," I tell her.

"So which baggie do you send? Even if they are 'animal' ashes and not vegetable or mineral, how do you know they all contain the same thing?"

"If I sent them all, they'd charge me for each one. We can't afford it."

Mira eyes clamp shut. Through her glasses her lids remind me of the surface of a desolate planet. Speculation is free, and infinite. In my heart of hearts, though, I've never really believed in the ancestry craze. It seems futile to look in the shadowy corners of your past for golden secrets.

My daughter-in-law comes to me again in a dream. I know it's Anna, even though her face is hidden behind a white veil. She's wearing a wedding dress that's also a hospital gown. Anna holds a bundle that I intuit is a baby, though I don't hear a sound or see an inch of exposed flesh. It's Thomas, of course. And now I see someone sitting some distance away on a beach chair: Jesse, though his face is turned away, focused, it seems, on the sun that's setting over an indigo sea. He's waiting for the green flash, I realize. A small campfire burns beside him—the air above the blaze wavers from the heat. The scent of scorched vanilla sears my nostrils. An indistinct figure rushes at me from outside the frame of my vision, and I see a raised machete. I lift my arm to absorb what seems like a certain blow, but the figure and the threat disappear instantly, and my deepest concern is that my hand now

THE VANISHING POINT MAGAZINE

blocks my view of the sun as it slips into the sea. Have I missed a glimpse of the green flash and lost my chance to discover the secrets of my own heart?

Silhouetted now against a rust-colored dusk are the children I no longer have: the young parents and their baby huddle beside the fire that burns red and flares with the steady throb of a heartbeat. Though my lips are sealed, my chest deflates as if I've gasped. No one in the shadow family returns my wave. Do they notice the little fires that rise from my knuckles instead of fingers? It's as if I'm holding up a fist of melting birthday candles. One by one the tiny flames wink out.

I wake up in bed beside my sleep-sighing wife. An image lingers of severed fingers blistering over an open fire. I lift my hand, but no matter how close I bring it to my face, I can't see it. It's too dark. I think I feel my fingers when I curl them into a fist, but I've heard too much about phantom limbs. I hypothesize: one finger per baggie? Half a finger? I wiggle my toes and feel my horny nails rasp against the sheet. Then I think to squeeze my shoulder, and I convince myself that I feel my fingertips dig into the meat of me.

Perhaps my ashes are sifting from a dream cloud at this very moment, black snow lost in the darkness, returning myself to myself in a continuous loop: ashes must rise before they fall. I wait in vain for dust to settle on my face. Where have Mira's dreams taken her? I reach toward her with my sleep-mutilated hand, then pause. What if her dream-fire burns more fiercely than mine and there's nothing left of my wife but her soughing breath? Can dream ash pile high enough to obliterate time?

The breakfast table, another morning—what else did you expect? In front of Mira and me are mugs of lukewarm coffee. Mira faces the window, and all I can see are her salt and pepper curls. She appears to be gazing out the window at the lawn, the trees, the river, the sky. Or perhaps she's lost in thought, reliving her own dreams.

"When is the last time either of us has talked to anybody?" I ask. "Besides each other? The mail comes, and we get new baggies. Groceries show up on the stoop once a week. But I don't recall speaking to a single soul."

Mira is silent for so long I wonder if I only thought my question. But finally my wife half-turns, presenting a profile like a cameo on a brooch.

"Have you started a list?" she asks. Her voice is muddy, as if she's underwater.

"List?"

"For the chain letter—where do you plan to send the ashes? Why didn't you ask for my opinion? I don't plan on being out of the loop."

"I'm not understanding you." My scalp tingles. I think of spiders.

"Why did you rearrange the letters on the refrigerator?" she asks. "I thought we agreed never to touch them. 'Let's leave everything to gravity,' you said."

"I said that?" I remember the thought, but not the discussion. Is this something she brought from a dream? I pivot for a look at the refrigerator. Craning my neck, I see the blots of color I know are the magnetic letters, but the only one I can identify with certainty is the *O*—the open, red-lipsticked mouth. The bloody hole.

"I can't see them. What do they say?"

"You spelled '*ASH TO*'—'Ash to' whom? Or to where?"

*Coincidence*, I try to say, but what comes out is "Ashtabula."  I've heard stories of corpses dead for days, that, when disturbed, belch out a final word.

"ASH-TUH-BOOLA," Mira pronounces carefully. "What's that? Is that a place?"

"It's a city in Ohio." I have no idea how or why I'm familiar with this fact, though I seem to know more: "It's on Lake Erie, not too far from Cleveland. 'Ashes for Ashtabula.'" I say it as if it's an advertising slogan.

"When were you thinking of telling me?" Mira slides her mug back and forth without lifting it. Her coffee sloshes with a plopping sound, but doesn't spill. "Do we know someone in Ashtabula? Tell me," she says wearily. "If we do, I don't remember. Anybody?"

"Nobody." I shrug like I'm trying on a jacket that's too tight. The morning light melts through the window, spreading across the table like a pool of warm butter. I sniff. "Are you baking cookies?"

"No. Why?"

Good question. At this point, I'm not sure what I do and don't know, which senses I can trust, which not. I inhale deeply: burnt vanilla! My dreams are leaking into my waking life like sawdust from a tear in an antique teddy bear. So much accumulating dust.

We will never send parts of ourselves to Ashtabula—or to any other city. We receive. We will dream in our beds, we will stare out this window, we will analyze the dust and ashes sent to us by the outside world. We will interpret and reinterpret the cryptic messages formed by the magnetic letters on our refrigerator. "*OM*" might become "*TOM*". Or "*MOT*," French for "word," which would have been there "in the beginning." France is where people go to see the green flash.

"Did Anna have eyes like lemurs?" Mira asks. "Sometimes in my dreams I picture little Thomas as a lemur with a human face. And sometimes he looks like a human infant with the face of a lemur. Do lemurs have green eyes?" I'm suddenly as cold as marble. This is the first time the name of our grandson has been spoken in this house since he failed to thrive.

"You're thinking of Madagascar," I say. "That's where lemurs live. Nobody we know has ever actually lived in Madagascar, remember?"

Mira turns back to the window. Its framed surface sizzles with the chaos of an untuned, old-fashioned television. I wince, as if I'm trying to find the 3D image hidden in one of those magic eye pictures. Out of a swirl of electric ash emerge the yard, the trees, the river, the sky, each distinct and neon-bright. Is that a family of three out there on the other side of the glass—a mother, a father, a toddler? I'm only just learning to see in this new world, where there's no distinction among past, present, and future; or between sleeping and waking. Maybe the family in my yard all have lemur eyes. Maybe I'm about to see their faces. Maybe I already have.

"If this is a chain," I hear Mira say, "if we're connected, we've got to offer something. We don't want to be out of the loop.

*Over one hundred of* **Gregory Wolos***'s short stories have been published in journals like Glimmer Train, Georgia Review, descant, Florida Review, The Pinch, Southern Humanities Review, Post Road, Nashville Review, Yemassee, Baltimore Review, Madison Review, The Doctor T. J. Eckleburg Review, Los Angeles Review, PANK, Superstition Review, and Tahoma Literary Review. His stories have earned numerous Pushcart Prize nominations and have won awards sponsored by descant, Solstice, the Rubery Book Awards, Gulf Stream, New South, Emrys Journal, and Gambling the Aisle. His full-length collections include Women of Consequence (Regal House Publishing, 2019), Dear Everyone (Duck Lake Books, 2020), and The Thing About Men (forthcoming, Cervena Barva Press, 2021). His debut novel, Kika Kong vs. the Dead White Males, will be*

*published by Adelaide Books in 2022. For full lists of his publications and com-mendations, visit* **www.gregorywolos.com**.

# RESILIENT CREATURES

*By J. Boyett*

S he awoke on the burnt-glass field. For a long time she lay curled on her side, holding her head, as if memories were physical things which might spill out. Like a disemboweled woman struggling to hold her guts in.

After a long time she could sit up. But only after she had sorted through her memories, all the decades and decades of life, putting them in some sort of order. They still didn't make sense. The winding paths were full of dead ends, strange doublings, the confused muzziness you'd expect after such a very, very long time. Memories of similar events chunked together. Some things, she feared to recall. Sequences were jumbled.

She remembered many, many times that she'd killed herself. She knew—or, anyway, she reasoned—that it was not *she* who had committed suicide; those selves were dead, annihilated. Only their minds had been recorded, to be implanted in the next cloned body. There had been a time when Barbara, to ease the trauma of those remembered self-murders, had argued philosophically that at least *that* Barbara's pain really had ended, and that since she herself was in a way that Barbara's sister, she should take comfort from her escape. All bullshit. Those Barbaras might have escaped from existence, but their memories had been grafted onto her mind, along with a sense of psychological continuity. All those suicides were *her* experiences now.

Of course, she could escape the same way they had. Probably, at least, if the Experiment let her. But she resolved to stay alive, for now. (Assuming this was life.) Not so much as a sentimental kindness to the future her, who did not exist yet and would not have to as long as Barbara stayed alive. Just because to kill herself would be something, and she couldn't see the point of doing *anything*.

Many memories. All the companions in pain who had come and

gone. Fiona. Peggy. Derek. Sibyl. Bryce. Ted, who she'd seen lifted up by an icy wind during a blizzard and slammed into the Razorfang Peaks—felt like fifty years ago. Once a group of them had all awoken together upon a tundra whose color hurt the eyes, and they'd watched Samantha's nude body melt, starting at the toes and ending at the crown, leaving only eyes in a puddle of gore and her gray hair. She screamed even after her lungs were melted, screamed till the bottom half of her face was gone. Had it been part of the Experiment, or had the new body been flawed? Barbara had never again seen any iteration of Samantha.

Lots of memories like that. Also of watching people starve or die of thirst. And of dying that way herself.

They hadn't really been "companions." Not for hundreds of years. Doesn't take much pain before your ability to give a fuck about your neighbor's trauma is burned away.

She looked up at the bruised sky. *I am in hell,* she thought listlessly, and decided she might as well stand up.

Naked this time. She looked at her body. Heavy, pendulous breasts; heavy thighs; a bit of a gut. She thought that in her life before, back in the human world, she'd weighed less, been more svelte.

She began to trudge. The gray-mottled black glass was warm; just blistered and irregular enough to give her a surface she could walk along without slipping, but not sharp enough to cut her feet. That little mercy made her nervous. Was she being set up for something worse? Off in the distance (she couldn't guess how far), the burnt-glass plain was bordered by a line of sheer ridges (she couldn't guess how high), stretching across the horizon.

She'd been trudging a while before she thought to look behind her and see what the terrain was like in the other direction. No reason to, really; there were never any meaningful choices. Nevertheless, she spent the energy necessary to turn in a half-circle.

And saw the red tower.

Sweeping up into the sky like a long red bone. A green light gleamed within the asymmetrical rounded knob of its summit.

Barbara could feel her lower lip fluttering. Her vision got smeary as her eyes moistened.

The red tower. Where it had all begun. (Maybe.) (She thought so.)

Those distant ridges were just more nothing. The tower, if real, might be something.

Far. When she'd first turned and seen it, it had loomed so huge in her mind that it had seemed she ought to be able to touch it. Now she saw that it must be many miles away. How long since she'd been there? How many centuries? Could have been a thousand years. She had accumulated more lived experiences than the human brain is designed to hold. That was part of why her memories were so confused.

The terrain in this direction grew less and less flat. The glass plain had buckled and bubbled in places before cooling, creating dips and shallows. Hiding places. Each time Barbara approached one the juices of her belly churned in terror of what she might find lurking there. Even after all these lifetimes, all these torments, she still retained the capacity to fear. Only fear was evergreen.

Peering over the lip of one such shallow she found the box staring back at her. With a shrill cry, she scrambled backwards. The glass here was rougher, with occasional edges, and Barbara stepped on one now and cut her sole before tumbling over and smacking first her backside, then her head. Before she could get up and run away, the thing called to her: "Barbara! No! It's me, Sibyl!"

Long ago, Barbara had learned that the mere fact of something knowing her name did not mean it was a friend. And the thing's voice was nothing like any voice of Sibyl's she'd ever heard; it was low, basso, belchy. And the fact that the thing identified itself as Sibyl was meaningless; the Experiment often called upon the environment to lie to her. But, once her body stopped shaking enough for her to do so, she heaved herself upright and went back to the thing, because if she wasn't going to kill herself then she may as well play the game.

"Sibyl?" she said, keeping her distance. Not that the thing seemed capable of movement.

"It's really me," belched Sibyl, in a voice so deep it was hard to make out the words. "I mean, I think it is."

The creature was a rectangular box of pink flesh, four feet long, three feet high, two feet deep. An oversized version of what really did look like Sibyl's usual face was smeared across the front. Patches of chestnut hair sprouted here and there from the pockmarked, mottled skin. A dozen huge warts were scattered across the front and sides, a wiry black bouquet springing from each.

This really was Sibyl, Barbara decided. It just seemed so much like the type of thing that would be done to one of them. "How long have you been here?"

Sibyl blew air out her mouth in a sigh. The gust of it hit Barbara and she might have vomited, if this body had been formed with food already in its belly. "Who knows," belched Sibyl. Her thick lips looked like ropes of ground beef, and Barbara noticed that they flapped slightly out of synch with her words.

Sibyl said she thought it had been weeks. She said she didn't sleep anymore and couldn't move, so it was hard to keep track.

From where Sibyl was wedged down in the shallow, it was impossible to see the red tower. So Barbara told her about it. But Sibyl already knew.

"I know lots of things now, that I can't know," she explained. "I think the Experiment decided it would be funny to make me a sibyl for real." For example, she told Barbara about the wheelbarrow just over the next rise, that Barbara could carry Sibyl in.

Barbara went to check. Sure enough, she saw a damn wheelbarrow, incongruous in this inhuman landscape. It looked beaten down by years of use. Barbara thought it probably had been created that way, but she supposed some other group of humans might have been forced to spend years performing some labor with it.

Perhaps it had even been her performing the labor. In some other iteration.

Barbara left the wheelbarrow and went back to look at Sibyl dubiously. "You look heavy," she said. "And the wheelbarrow looks ready to fall apart. And the ground is rough, between here and the red tower."

"You have to take me with you."

"Why?" Centuries ago, Barbara would have been ashamed to ask such a question even silently, would have hidden it away inside her. Even after their arrival here in the Experiment, the decency conditioning she'd received from her upbringing in the human world had taken some time to crack.

"Because it's meant to be. I know. I told you, I really am a sibyl now."

Barbara only looked at her with flat dull eyes. They'd spent too long in the Experiment to believe that anything was "meant to be."

She said, "This is the red tower." What she meant was she wouldn't take on any burden that might keep her from reaching the tower. She was going to add, *I might be able to get out of here,* but realized she wouldn't be able to say it without her voice trembling. And she didn't want the Experiment to overhear, even though she was sure it knew her thoughts.

"Please," begged Sibyl. A horrible sound, in that big deep voice. "It's not bullshit. The Experiment put knowledge in my head. I know things about you now. And the tower. Leave me here and I won't tell you what they are."

"How do you know any of the things the Experiment put in your head are true?" But Barbara went to get the wheelbarrow without waiting for an answer. Not that she cared what Sibyl might know about her. But maybe there would be something about the tower that she could use.

She brought the wheelbarrow as close as she could to the lip of the shallow. Even that was hard. And wrestling Sibyl up the glassy slope was a hell of a job. Barbara gripped her at her edges and felt an alarming give to the bone frame of this box of flesh. What would happen if Sibyl's new body fell apart? The flesh had a moist, oily feel, and a smell like old mayonnaise. It was maybe a hundred pounds. A couple times Barbara dropped her during the short climb. Turned out Sibyl's latest body did have nerves and pain receptors—she cried out. Once Barbara dropped her on a jagged patch of glass and tore Sibyl's skin. The maroon blood oozed out, very thick.

Barbara got Sibyl settled into the wheelbarrow, facing front so that she could see the tower and also so that Barbara wouldn't have to smell her breath. She shoved the wheelbarrow forward, wrestling with it through the hard landscape. Its sullen blankness seemed to stretch to eternity. What was this landscape? Perhaps Barbara and Sibyl and their surroundings were mere computer simulations. But this *seemed* like a physical place.

Anyway. It had been many centuries since she'd cared. She only still thought of it sometimes because her synapses insisted on sparking in their old, accustomed patterns.

Barbara wanted to ask if any of these things Sibyl supposedly knew could help them escape via the tower, which was how they'd entered the Experiment. (Barbara was *almost* sure of that, even though those memories were foggy and muddled.) But she couldn't ask that yet. The hope frightened her too badly. Probably this view of the tower was merely another subset of the Experiment, one that in its way was crueler than, say, the time slug eggs had hatched inside her ears, and the slugs had squeezed their way further and further into her head until she'd died.

So instead of asking about the tower she tried a version of small talk. Asked, when had been the last time they'd seen each other? She meant under what circumstances; useless to try to determine how long it had been in terms of decades.

Sibyl replied, "That swamp. With the poison yellow flowers. We ate a bad fish. It paralyzed us. Four-inch crimson ants came and ate our legs. Not the rest of us, though. The paralysis wore off but without our legs it was hard to move. We starved to death."

Barbara didn't say anything. Wasn't a pleasant memory. The crimson ants had had some sort of acid in their mandibles that had cauterized the wound of each bite. But Sibyl was wrong. "That wasn't the last time," Barbara said. "That was long, long ago. The last time for you and me was that blizzard. We got separated in the snow."

Barbara could tell from her tone that Sibyl would have shaken her head if she'd had one. "Your subjective memories are all screwed up. That's part of the stuff I know now." Barbara didn't reply but did reflect that it took no special wisdom to know *that*. But then Sibyl said, "All the memories you're carrying. They don't even belong to one continuous self. Experiences of different clone lineages have been spliced together, out of order. Whole mess has been dumped into your head. You have nine-hundred-seventy-three years, four months, eight days, twelve minutes' worth of subjective memories."

Nine-hundred-seventy-three years. It seemed like she should be crazier, after all that time. The Experiment must be manipulating her mind that way, too. Keeping her psyche artificially stapled into one piece. Not even her own madness was she allowed to have.

Barbara marched along without speaking. Ever since she had first realized that she was reawakening in cloned bodies with copied memories, it had occurred to her that there might be other versions of herself out there at the same time, elsewhere in the vastness of the Experiment. But it had never occurred to her that she might receive the memories of clones whose memory lineages had diverged. Or no, actually, she realized, she *had* thought of that. But then it seemed once again that she hadn't. And then she realized that she was accessing different sets of memories, from different clone lineages. Memories that had been snarled together out of sequential order.

She'd had time to grow accustomed to her memories being distorted in other ways. Her memories of her life before, in the human world, had always been available only in snatches. Her memories of her arrival here, via the red tower, had always been partial and visible only through a translucent barrier. She'd never been able to remember exactly how or why she'd come....

Except that wasn't true either. While she currently had no access to that knowledge, she did remember having known it in the past. And she remembered not having liked what she'd known.

Sibyl said, "I'll tell you something else that I know. Or that I think I know. The way into the red tower is open, and there are no guards."

Barbara shivered. She managed to keep pushing the rickety wheelbarrow along. "And once we get inside? Is there a ... a door on the other side? A door that will let us out?"

"Hmpf. Maybe. But I'll tell you what I do see. The quantum server in which all copies of your mind are stored. It's there. And next to that, a sledgehammer."

"But ... why? Why would the Experiment give me access to those?"

"Maybe this is the Experiment's final phase. Will you kill yourself for real? With no chance of resurrection? Maybe they want to learn if endless suffering has made your will to survive perversely stronger. Or maybe the Experiment's funding has been pulled and they want to wrap it up."

Barbara didn't try to keep the tremble from her voice: "You mean they'll let us end it? Really end it?"

"Not *us*." Sibyl's voice was bitter. "It's only *your* mind that's there. Or so they tell me."

---

Took a long time to get to the tower. Who knows how long. This time, their bodies had no need to eat, sleep, shit, or piss, so there was nothing to mark the time. Not even the growth of hunger, or thirst. The sun never moved.

But they arrived. Sibyl wept when she saw the flimsy ladder that climbed to the entrance, twenty feet above the ground. Black tears like machine oil dripped in straight lines down the meaty plane of her face. "I hoped it would be stairs," she spat. "If it had been stairs I would have begged you to carry me up with you. Can't you try to hold me? While you climb the ladder?"

"No. I can't take you. It's not possible."

Sibyl's breath wheezed in and out of what Barbara supposed must be lungs. The obscene pink cords of her lips knotted in hate and self-pity. "I knew they wouldn't let me out. I just wanted to see it again. I just wanted to see where it all started."

Barbara hesitated at the base of the ladder. Sibyl would be utterly helpless and immobile, alone in that body. Barbara scanned the ground. No stones, no loose shards, nothing she could use to knock loose a chunk of glass. Still, she went ahead and asked, "Do you want me to kill you? I could try to figure something out."

"No. It wouldn't make any fucking difference."

Barbara left her. The entrance at the top of the ladder was only a black slit cut into the wall. Before she stepped inside, she spared a last glance down at Sibyl. The face messily stamped onto the box of flesh was big enough that even from up here, Barbara could make out its sullen features. It didn't look like an animated thing. She wondered how long Sibyl would sit in that wheelbarrow, staring at the tower. If that body really didn't need to eat or drink, it could be a hundred years. Could be forever. Barbara slipped the rest of the way into the dark doorway, without waving goodbye. It wasn't like Sibyl could wave back.

Within, all was pitch black. The floor inclined up. Barbara knew, from running her fingertips along the unseen walls of the narrow corridor, that there were no openings into other chambers, no chance to take a different turn. Only one way to go.

The hallway twisted its way up the tower. Her feet pushed her body along the mild incline. The floor and walls were of the same material: solid, granular stone. Her breathing sounded loud in the still darkness, and she was aware of its irregularity. It seemed to her that nothing had ever been quite as frightening as the possibility that a way out might be up ahead. Possibly only meters distant. A way out that could be suddenly snatched away.

The darkness began to glow dimly. Barbara told herself it was her imagination, or else a trick. Then she rounded a final curve and stopped short. Before her she beheld a rectangle outlined in light. She had to cast around in her memories before identifying the thing: a door.

How many centuries since she had seen a door?... Well, almost nine and a half, according to Sibyl.

She raised her palms and held them out. It was dark enough that she wasn't sure her body had obeyed her until she felt the rough texture of the door against her vibrating flesh. She pushed. The door fell open.

She swallowed her hyperventilation and stepped over the threshold.

Looking around the room she began to sob. She wanted to cry, *I re-*

*member! I remember!*

A desk, bare. A chair. File cabinets! Christ Almighty, when had she last thought about file cabinets! And a sledgehammer, propped against the wall, and beside that a white humming box that just had to be the quantum server.

Also, there was a person.

The person was a woman. Dressed, in the kinds of clothes Barbara knew she had once considered normal. These types of clothes remained fresh in her consciousness because from time to time, following its own whims, the Experiment had resurrected her clad in their like, or with a supply nearby: blouse with frilled front, sweater, knee-length floral skirt, pumps. The woman's hair was a helmet of ashen curls. Terrified, she was pressing herself back against the gray cinder-block wall, fist to her mouth as she gnawed the knuckle, wild eyes fixed on Barbara.

Barbara blinked in surprise. All of a sudden she realized that this was her. That was her body, or what her body used to look like, originally.

"You're *naked,*" said the other her, as if this were the one horror she'd never anticipated.

Barbara took another step into the room, still blinking. Even the sledgehammer and the quantum server were momentarily forgotten in the shock of meeting this other iteration of herself.

The other Barbara scooted back and forth along the wall, as if eventually she would find a way past that barrier and be able to put even more space between herself and Barbara. "I waited," she babbled, "I waited and I waited, and they told me to stand guard, and I did, and I'm here."

Something Barbara's eyes had skipped over during their first sweep caught her attention now: a square upon the wall, filled with smaller squares, many of them X'ed out. Atop the square, a word: AUGUST. Barbara took a step toward it, awed. Her voice breathed out, "*Calendar,*" tongue fondling the long-disused word.

"*You stay away from that!*" The other Barbara sprang at her, nails out, then leaped back against the wall, losing her nerve. Flattening herself against the wall again, she glared at Barbara, teeth bared. "*Don't you touch that!* I've been keeping track! Counting the days! They'll know how long it's been. How long I've been here. I'll need to know that, when I sue! And I'll need to know it for when I show them how good I've been. How good. How good. How good."

"'Sue.'" A word she'd once known, but Barbara couldn't remember what it meant.

She gave the other iteration a fresh look. The woman seemed mad, of course. But the flavor of her insanity was different from Barbara's, from Sibyl's. Barbara felt a sudden thrum of intuition: *This one hasn't been out in the Experiment.* She'd been in this room. Alone, and for a long time—that was how she'd gone crazy. Even so, Barbara couldn't help but look down a little on anyone who could be so weak as to go crazy despite having the luxury of a calendar, and one body to live in while you marked off the days so you could be sure there weren't any gaps.

Barbara took a step towards the other iteration. Her other self startled away with a whimper; Barbara took a second step. Although she'd suspected there might be other iterations of herself wandering the Experiment, and now had memories of various iterations crammed together in her head, she'd never before come face-to-face with a version of herself. (Not that she could remember, anyway.)

"Who are you?" asked Barbara.

The other version hesitated, as if trying to gauge whether it would be dangerous to answer. "I'm Barbara McCullough."

Barbara felt at a loss. She had asked the wrong question somehow; she tried again: "What's happened to you?"

The question flipped her doppelganger back from fear into rage. "I'll fucking, I'll fucking, I'll fucking sue! Just a quick trip to their office, they say, just a quick trip to their lab! Just a small donation of genetic material! Just half an hour for the mind-scan!"

Barbara nearly lost her footing, as if the floor had tilted. But it was within herself that things were tilting. Shocked, she realized that this woman retained all her memories of the human world, of the life there from before the Experiment. "Are you... are you the original?" she gasped. "How long have you been here?"

The woman's face balled up like a used and dried-out Kleenex. "More than a *year*! They told me to wait here, and that someone would come! They told me to watch over that, too, to protect it if anyone tried to, to destroy it." She was pointing at the quantum server.

Barbara frowned. True, all those spliced and crammed-together memories had artificially padded her sense of how much time had passed. But no way this process had begun merely a year ago. It took a moment for the obvious solution to dawn on her: this was another clone. But she had been awakened with all the memories of the original Barbara McCullough, and since she'd never died and been reborn she had no reason to believe she *wasn't* the original.

It sounded like her memories of the human world were clearer than Barbara's. Like she might know something about the nature of the Experiment.

"What is it?" Barbara took another step and held out her hand. The gesture was meant to be supplicatory but the fingers curled like claws. "What did I do?" The other iteration blinked, and Barbara realized that the question, thus phrased, made no sense; it should be "What did *we* do?" or, better still, "What did *you* do?," since it was the other iteration's memories that she hoped to access.

All of a sudden it felt like something clotted within her had come unstuck. For all these lifetimes, she'd had the sense (and sometimes, she thought, the certain knowledge) that her entry here, however it had happened, had been her fault. But why should she take responsibility any longer? Her mind was too garbled now for her to share a true continuity with the original Barbara McCullough. But this woman did.

That made it all *her* fault. Close enough, anyway.

"What did you do?" she asked.

"I didn't do *anything*! I just showed up for the appointment! They took a tissue sample. Just a scraping from my mouth. Then the mind scan— I fell asleep during that. And when I woke up I was here! And I haven't seen anyone in a year!"

"If you haven't seen anyone, who told you to defend the quantum server?"

Barbara frowned. Her own confusion frightened her. "I … I don't remember exactly.… *Someone* did! And anyway that's not the point! They can't do this to me!"

Memories were coming unstuck in Barbara—nothing very clear, and even as they surfaced to her view she still thought of them as the other Barbara's fault. As belonging to her. "They can do whatever they want because you signed a contract with them, you stupid bitch!"

"Not one that said they could do whatever they wanted with me! Just one that said they could run experiments on my genetic material!"

"You *are* the genetic material!… What is it for? The Experiment?"

"What do you care?"

*"What are they experimenting on us for?!"*

The other iteration flinched. "Something about, uh, I think it was about, um, stressors. Just, like, the human psyche's reactions to negative stimuli, they said. And positive stimuli."

Positive stimuli? Barbara certainly had zero memory of those. "What did you get?" she demanded. "What did they give you? In exchange for the tissue sample and the mind scan?"

"A hundred dollars." The other iteration blinked back tears. "And I never even got to spend it!"

A hundred dollars. Barbara remembered money. She tried to remember what you could get for a hundred dollars. Not a lot, she thought.

She studied the other woman, who was so close to really being Barbara McCullough. A hell of a lot closer than Barbara herself was. Nothing much had apparently been done to her mind, after all, except if you counted the effects of leaving her alone in this room for a year. That didn't seem so bad.

Barbara McCullough had gotten a hundred dollars for what had been done to them. It must have seemed like a pretty good deal. Stop by the lab —get a mouth swab—take a half-hour nap under the mind scanner—then drive home.

If they really were simulations in a server, Barbara McCullough might not even have left the lab yet. Centuries of memories might be generated by an AI within nanoseconds. Perhaps it had still been less than a second since Barbara McCullough had regained consciousness under the scanner. Perhaps she hadn't even sat up yet.

The server.

Barbara looked at the smooth humming white box. And at the sledgehammer.

She marched across the room with more purpose than she'd felt in a very long time. Grabbed the sledgehammer. At first she feared it would be too heavy for the noodly muscles of her arms. But she got it hefted up onto her shoulders.

Reactions delayed, and not daring to get close, the other iteration held out her arms. "Wait—I have to protect that! They told me to protect that. I'm scared of what they'll do if I don't protect it."

Barbara turned. Heaved the sledgehammer up over her head. Brought it down on the humming white box. It made a slapping bang, like the box was protesting such treatment.

Had no other effect, though.

Barbara went nuts. Shrieking, she attacked the server, swinging the sledgehammer into it from both sides, raising it overhead and letting it drop onto the box. When her strength gave out she let the sledgehammer fall and started kicking the server. Broke three toes. She punched it, slapped it. Bit it.

Then she was on her knees before it, face on the cold linoleum. Tears and snot expelled themselves from her face as she sobbed. The server bore not a mark. Its cool surface and quiet hum was a reminder that calmness could exist in the universe.

Barbara regained enough self-control to wipe off her face with her hand and raise her gaze. At first she didn't know why she bothered. Then she saw the other iteration, and remembered she was there.

The other iteration, cringing against the wall, stared at her. "I'm supposed to be protecting that," she rasped.

Barbara worked herself back upright. Managed to pick up the sledgehammer. Held it out towards the other iteration. "Here. Please hit me in the head with this until I die."

"No!" The other iteration shrank back even more, as if *she* were the one being threatened.

"Please. I'm done with this round. The Experiment isn't going to let us out."

"No!" The other iteration's face screwed up again and she started once more to cry. "No! No! No! I can't! Please go away again and leave me alone! I waited so long for someone to come, but it was better when I was alone!"

The sledgehammer grew too heavy to hold. Barbara rested its big head on the floor. She regarded the other woman. It was true what she said —she couldn't. Not yet. Only a year old, she hadn't been cycled through enough yet. Wasn't tough enough yet.

Suddenly Barbara saw that the other iteration was like a little sister, who needed taking care of. "Okay. Don't worry then. I'll do it, this time." Somehow she managed to get the sledgehammer back up over her shoulder. The other iteration's reflexes were slow, and she didn't even duck as Barbara smashed the hammer into the side of her face. On the floor, she croaked in mournful protest. "Don't worry," said Barbara. "You'll go to sleep. Someone else will wake up, but it won't be you."

Later, the other iteration's headless corpse lay beside a wet patch of blood, brain, cerebrospinal fluid, bone meal, and crushed linoleum. Barbara sat with her back against the cool, vibrating server, waiting to die. Maybe something would come to kill her. If not, dying could take years. Could take forever.

Positive stimuli, the other iteration had said. Were there yet more iterations of herself, of Sibyl, of Fiona, of Ted, iterations living eternities of Paradise as she lived eternities of Hell? She tried to gauge whether it hurt her, the idea that it had been only the luck of the draw that had kept her from awakening in such a place as that. But she didn't give a shit. Their distant pleasures or pains had nothing to do with her. Hell is a lonely place.

A hundred dollars had been paid to Barbara McCullough. If Barbara was a physically existent clone in a super-massive enclosure, or a fairly massive one equipped with high-level VR, then that had been decades or centuries ago. If Barbara was merely data in a quantum server, then it could have been less than a second. Either way, it had been a long, long time.

Things you could get for a hundred dollars: A few nights out at the movies. Fancy underwear. Nachos with some friends.

*J. Boyett*, *currently residing in Brooklyn, has had stories published in* Sensitive Skin *and a play,* Poisoned, *published by Next Stage Press.* Boyett *is also the author of several novels, including* Ironheart, The Switch, *and* The Sexbot.

# SUPER BOWL SUNDAY

*By Michaele Jordan*

**B**ut Jerry," sighed Michelle. "You don't even like football!" There was a long silence. "Do you? You said you didn't." She pouted. She certainly didn't like football. But the pout (a very pretty one, actually) was wasted on Jerry. The weather was bad—they really should have stayed home—and he had to keep his eyes on the road.

Jerry sighed. "Look, you've been hinting like you want to meet the family. So you want to meet the family or not? 'Cause this is your last chance 'til next Thanksgiving." She pouted some more. She had been hinting that she'd like to meet the family. That didn't mean she wanted to watch football. "And it's not like anybody's going to make you watch the game. Lots of the girls don't." He managed a quick glance her way and finally saw the pretty pout. "You know my Aunt Karen makes the best chili in the world." The car skidded, but he was a good driver and braked gently into it. When balance was restored, he continued firmly, "It's worth the trip. Really. Even if you hate football."

Michelle chewed on her lip. She was not entirely unaware that Jerry wasn't really being unreasonable. But he had no idea what a chill it sent up her spine when he said, "Lots of the girls don't." She, too, had grown up in a home where the women hung out in the kitchen and the men watched TV in the family room. She had hated it. She had really hated it.

She shook her head. She was being petty and mean. She cared for Jerry. He really was the sweetest guy in the world; it wouldn't kill her to sit through one game. She forced herself to smile. "The chili's good?"

"MICHELLE!" She was swept up in a bear hug before she had entirely figured out who was speaking. Peering out over the shoulder against which she was suddenly squished she saw Jerry roll his eyes and make a "Hey, what can you do?" gesture. "Oh, dear, am I overdoing the warm hospitality thing?" The warm, hospitable person backed off a step or two, so Michelle could see a tall, handsome, forty-odd woman with lots of ridiculous pepper-and-salt lamb curls and deep set, penetrating grey eyes. "I'm sorry. You don't know how we've been nagging Jerry to get you here. I'm Karen. Great to meet you." Karen offered a large hand and a strong handshake.

"Jerry's mentioned me?" She got a huge laugh. This was very good. The bear hug had been a little scary, but Jerry talking her up to the family was good.

"Naw," said Jerry. He got a big laugh, too.

Karen wrapped an arm around her and swept her off to the kitchen. "Introductions later. Just call everybody sweetie. You must be chilled to the bone—let's get you something hot. Can you believe this weather?" Karen poured a big mug of dark, steaming coffee. Without even asking, she laced it with cream—not milk, real cream—and two spoons of sugar.

Michelle reached for it gratefully, but hands—probably friendly—gently drew her back to pull off her coat and hat. She was turned around in the process and found herself facing two tall, matching teenagers. Both wore fuzzy sweaters over inadequate little tube tops that would have concealed very little, even if there had been anything much to conceal. Their identical faces were topped with nearly identical lamb curls—like Karen's, only purple.

"Yes," said the twins. "We're twins." The scary thing was that both pairs of lips moved; Michelle had no idea which one had spoken. "Dana," and "Donna," continued the twins. "We'll just take your hat and coat." They already had. "Oh, no! Your boots are all wet! They'll be ruined." The two faces turned to face each other, almost nose to nose. "We better get her some slippers." They turned and sped away in exactly opposite directions, like two charged atomic particles.

"Thanks, D," she called after them, wondering if she would ever see her hat and coat again.

"Don't let the twins bother you," said a round, smiling little blond woman. "They're such brats—they live to mess with people's minds. And the only way to stop them...."

"Is to pretend not to notice," finished Michelle. "The nature of the teen beast." She extended a hand. "I'm...."

"Yeah, I know. Save your breath—we all know. I'm Carol. Bob's sister."

"My husband," chirped Karen.

"Jerry's other aunt," continued Carol; her handshake was soft but sincere. Michelle decided she liked her.

"Come eat," interjected Karen, handing her that gorgeous cup of coffee—which tasted so good Michelle forgot to ask how Karen had known how she took it. "You should know," continued Karen, waving at another round, blond lady that looked a lot like Carol. "This is my other sister-in-law, Jenny. She'll be wounded if you don't try the Swedish meatballs."

"Unless you're a vegetarian," Jenny assured her, taking her arm and almost dragging her to the buffet. "Which would be all right. We've got tons of veggies, and Maggie made fondue. You're not vegan, are you?"

Michelle didn't answer. She was gaping at the food. The first tier was just sandwich fixings, except there was nothing 'just' about it. There was chicken, roast beef and ham, of course. But there was also corned beef and pastrami, pancetta and prosciutto and salami. There was baby Swiss, pepper jack and horseradish cheddar, baguettes and three kinds of bread, mostly homemade. The tomato slices looked fresh, though where they got fresh tomatoes this time of year, Michelle couldn't guess. There were pitas and hummus and babaghanoush, in case the dreaded vegan showed up. Behind the sandwich makings stood a whole phalanx of crock-pots: Jenny's Swedish meatballs, and Karen's chili, creamed chipped beef and chicken noodle soup and Maggie's fondue. Plus another crock-pot of roast beef, kept hot and juicy. "How many people are coming?" asked Michelle, a little faintly.

"Just family," said Jenny (or was it Carol?). "Maybe twenty-five, not counting kids." She misinterpreted the look on Michelle's face. "Hey, it's not as bad as it looks. Really. We've got lots of healthy stuff," she pointed to a fruit bowl the size of the Houston Astro-Dome ranked by a thousand salads. "And some of this is low-fat. But it's cold out—we figured we needed a little comfort food."

She was right, of course, and Michelle was already drooling, although she couldn't help wondering about the dishes. But she was a guest; she wouldn't have to do any dishes. "I'll start with the Swedish meatballs," she announced. "Can't risk hurt feelings." Jenny grinned. It had to be Jenny.

"Excuse me." A clone of Alice-in-Wonderland tugged on her elbow. "I brought you some slippers." The child held up two large, fuzzy pink things, presumably as evidence. "Mom says these'll fit you."

"But...." said Michelle.

Carol stood on tiptoe to whisper in her ear. "Just go along, Michelle. You're dealing with Barb."

"But...." said Michelle. Carol pressed her down into a chair that had materialized behind her. Barb's daughter pulled off her boots. And the boots really hurt. She'd been ten pounds lighter when she bought them. Since she was sitting, Jenny handed her a plate of Swedish meatballs. They were delicious.

"There you are!" Jerry appeared at the doorway, accompanied by two men and three women. "Everything all right?" He stopped and surveyed the food. "Wow." He turned to the tall guy in the green flannel shirt. "Frank, why is everybody hanging out in the family room? Have they no values?" He built a sandwich and grabbed a bowl of chili.

"They're watching the game?" suggested the woman in the horrible horn-rimmed glasses and the cable knit sweater.

The other man—balding, in a striped long sleeve polo—rolled his eyes. "The game won't start for another twenty minutes, Susan."

"But they have to stake out their territories," pointed out the woman in the posh silk top. Her hair cut looked expensive, too. "Except for Bob, it's first come first served, if you want a real chair. They don't even dare go to the bathroom." She helped herself to chicken noodle soup. "Hi, I'm Barb."

"Oops," said Jerry. "I forgot introductions. Sorry. This is Susan and Barbara." So she was the mother of the blond child.

"My daughter," chirped Karen. There was no particular resemblance.

"And Maggie." Maggie wore jeans and a grey t-shirt that said, "Voodoo Jazz, New Orleans 1992" and pictured dozens of little skulls. "And this is Frank..."

"My son," added Karen.

Jerry waved that off and pointed to the guy who knew when the game would start. "And this is Mike. He's with Susan. Pay attention to his shirt. Sooner or later you'll meet Mark—that's Jenny's husband—and they're identical twins."

"Does that mean Donna and Dana are yours?" guessed Michelle. She'd heard that twins ran in families.

Susan smiled, a tight little smile. "Donna and Dana are Mark and Jenny's grandchildren." Michelle looked back to Jenny and guessed her age upward ten years.

"Have you met Grandma yet?" inquired Jerry, spooning diced onions, grated cheese and crackers into a second bowl of chili.

It sounded like an innocent question to Michelle, but dead silence fell. "I don't think so."

"We thought we'd feed her first," explained Karen, like she thought it needed explaining.

"What for?" said Mike. "No point getting attached to her until we find out if we can keep her." He chuckled, but with a sour note. No one else laughed. Michelle did some mental arithmetic. Karen was Jerry's aunt because she was married to Jerry's uncle, Bob. Jenny was Bob's sister and was married to Mark, Mike's brother. So, Mike and Susan weren't really relatives. Just in-laws. Judging by the looks everybody was giving them, that mattered. She turned to Jerry. If things worked out between them, was she going to be just another in-law? Everybody had seemed so friendly.

Jerry put down his chili. "You know, he's got a point," he replied casually. Had he really not noticed the undertones? "What do you say, Michelle? You ready to meet the queen of the hive?"

"I don't know, Jerry. If she doesn't like me, do I have to walk home?" She kept the tone light, and everybody laughed. Jerry gave her his I-really-like-you-smile and formally offered her his arm. He looked a question to his Aunt Karen who smiled.

"She's holding court in the conservatory."

"Aren't you even going to warn her?" inquired Susan with another tight little smile.

Jerry sighed. "Okay." So, he didn't like Susan either. Barb finished her soup and drifted out of the kitchen. Jenny rushed off to check on her meatballs. Karen just looked at Susan. "Listen. There's a fifty-fifty chance Grandma will tell you she's a witch."

Michelle's heart skipped and stopped. Foolish. She nibbled another meatball.

"Aren't you going to ask?" murmured Susan. Her smile just got tighter and tighter.

Michelle decided she didn't like Susan either. "Ask what?" she inquired with big innocent eyes. Karen chuckled. Michelle put down her empty meatball plate and took Jerry's arm. His I-really-like-you-smile got even bigger and they walked away. They walked down a long hall past a lot of rooms. It was a really big house.

"Don't get bent out of shape about the witch thing. Please. Grandma's just a little old lady," he whispered in her ear. Interesting. He didn't say 'wacky'.

The conservatory wasn't as cold as she expected. Had to be double paned glass. And there was an adorable little Swedish wood stove. And— oh, God, of course—a whole bunch more people. It really did look like a court. Jerry's Mom, she knew from the pictures, and one of the pictures had included that big guy with the Leonard Bernstein hair. So that would be Uncle Bob. The young one that looked just like Jerry would be his sister, Lynne. And the walking mummy had to be Grandma. Plus three 'sweeties'. She braced herself.

But the three sweeties bowed right out with a whisper of names: Debbie, Linda, Margo. Bob shook her hand like he meant never to let go and shepherded off Lynne and Mom. And Jerry. Within minutes, she was alone with the witch.

Michelle looked around. The ceiling lights created a bright, warm little bubble, snugly enclosed within the leaden skies and blowing snow plainly visible outside. There were plants ranked along the windows, sur- prisingly green for dead of winter, not that Michelle knew anything about plants. There were Planters' chairs and wicker tables scattered around a Navajo rug on a nice, tile floor. Grandma looked even worse close up than she had from a distance. But her eyes were sharp.

Grandma watched her look around with an amused twist at the corner of her leathery lips. Michelle smiled. "I'm very pleased to meet you, Ma'am. Thanks for inviting me—you have a beautiful home."

Grandma burst out laughing, which was not the reaction Michelle had been hoping for. "Right. Of course. You're very welcome, child."

Okay, it was like that. "Everybody says I'm in trouble if you don't like me. I'm almost afraid to tell you I'm a terrible cook and not much better at dishes."

Grandma laughed again, which was good. This time Michelle had meant her to laugh. "What else did they tell you about me?"

"That you tell people you're a witch."

"How do you feel about that?"

Michelle shrugged. "My grandmother told people she was a witch, too. But she wasn't." That worked. Grandma sat up straighter.

"How do you know?"

She shrugged again. "That's a beautiful housecoat, Ma'am." She hadn't been asked to drop the 'Ma'am'. "Is it real silk?"

Grandma stared at her hard. A long time. Finally, she smiled and nodded. "It is, child. I take it your grandmother didn't have a silk housecoat."

"No, Ma'am. She wore polyester and she lived in a trailer. She drank too much, and she died young. Stomach cancer—a terrible way to go. But right up to the end, everybody was afraid of her." Michelle looked around again, from the imported tile to the gorgeous Persian runner in the hall— just visible through the door—and back to Grandma's silk housecoat. The babble of conversation drifting in from the family room rose suddenly to a crescendo and stopped cold. The game must be starting. Michelle sighed. "You really do have a beautiful home, Ma'am." She smiled. "Maybe you are a witch. Why didn't you like Mark?"

Grandma blinked. "My goodness, you have been fitting right in. It was nothing personal. But he couldn't give Jenny children. And he didn't tell Jenny that. So, she didn't believe me when I told her. She was gone a long time until she figured it out."

"But then she came back, and you fixed it for her?" Because Jenny had grandchildren.

"Didn't have to. They got help. Modern technology really is amazing." Grandma smiled. "The treatments were really rough on Jenny. But she had her family to help her through it."

"And Susan."

"Well, that was another downside to Mark. I suppose your grandmother would have had her killed. Do you garden?"

"Beg pardon?"

"You don't cook. Do you garden? Or knit? Throw pots? Build cabinets? Something creative?"

"I sing in the choir."

"Ah, yes, the arts. Very nice. But can you actually make anything?"

Michelle reminded herself that Grandma was nearly ninety. Or maybe even a hundred. "Does making money count?"

"You make good money?"

"Six figures, Ma'am." Not that it was any business of hers.

Grandma nodded. "At your age? That's creative. Are you fertile?"

"As far as I know." She thought about Mark. "Would it be that bad if I weren't?"

"Yes. Definitely. Power is recessive. None of my kids have it. They must carry it, but most of their spouses don't have it either. I really got my hopes up when Bob married Karen. What she does with plants isn't natural. I mean, homegrown tomatoes in January? But their kids don't have any power either. But you do; I can smell it. I don't see what you're doing with it, but you've got it. So, there's a good chance your kids will, too."

"What about the little blond girl?" Karen and Bob's granddaughter. "Maybe it skips a generation. Like the twinning."

Grandma nodded. "Like you." Michelle shook her head emphatically. "I'm watching Paula. Carefully. In the meanwhile, I think you and Jerry should get married."

Michelle almost wished she didn't like Jerry so much so she could refuse. "He hasn't asked me."

"He will at half time." A chorus of hoots and cheers rose up from the family room. Grandma turned to look at the door back into the main house. "Sounds like the game's going well. Why don't you go watch it with Jerry? It's getting chilly in here, anyway." She gathered a cashmere shawl around her.

"I hate football."

Grandma laughed until she started to cough. "It'll grow on you. I know, it's a stupid game. But year after year, you sit around with family, eating the food—the boys all cheering, the girls laughing. You trade stories, make memories. You get grateful for that stupid game."

"So you're saying I have to come all the way out here every year, in weather like this, for a stupid game?" Michelle forced a smile that was almost as tight as Susan's.

Grandma shrugged. "I notice you weren't here for Christmas. Thanksgiving either." Michelle thought about that. Even if she did marry Jerry, she probably wouldn't be able to come for Christmas. Sure, it was a great house and good people (well, mostly), but she had relatives of her own, some of them troubled maybe, but still hers.

"It's not just you," continued Grandma. "They've all got other families, places they have to go on the regular holidays. And that's good. I'm not in the business of breaking up families. Instead, I gather them here for a blessing every Super Bowl Sunday. And you know what? Little Jimmy told me it's his very favorite holiday." She chuckled. "Boys just love games, you know. And if you love the boy, you live with a few games."

The two women faced each other in a long, thoughtful silence. Michelle wasn't going to break it. She'd learned a long time ago that it always paid off to make the other guy talk first.

"You like the house, Michelle? You give Jerry a child, a child with Power, and I'll leave the house to you. You think I care if you cook?"

It was a really good deal, even if the house was a long way out of town. The only serious downside was the old lady herself. And that was such a short-term problem. She was old, older than even her children realized, and she had hardly any time left. She was barely going to live long enough to change her will.

Michelle smiled her very best smile and rose. "Don't worry, Grandma." She crossed to the old woman and kissed her flaking, wrinkled cheek. "I'll give Jerry four children, and they'll all have Power." She took the old woman's hand and caressed it gently. "But I don't know how to prove that to you. It takes a while for the Power to show up. You can't tell when they're babies." She softened the blow slightly. "I'm not sure you'll live long enough to watch them grow up."

Grandma's eyes widened slightly. "You mean you're pretty sure I won't. Will I see the first one born?"

"Sure, you will," said Michelle. "And he'll have Power. So, I get the house?"

And Grandma smiled. "I believe you. You get the house." There were more rowdy noises in the family room.

Michelle pressed her hand gently and let go. As she walked away, Grandma's eyes grew very wide, and she coughed and choked. She laid a withered hand on her shriveled breast and looked up with an open mouth to watch Michelle go. Michelle didn't actually see it, but then, she didn't need to.

Jerry was waiting in the hallway, just inside the door. "How'd it go?"

"Oh, Jerry. She's an absolute doll! We got along great!" She took his hand and offered him a mischievous grin. "You know what she said? She said you were going to ask me to marry you at half time!"

Jerry laughed and laughed. "Joke's on her. I'm not waiting until half time." He drew her into his arms for a long, satisfying kiss. Behind them, there was another unhappy, frightened little cough, but Jerry didn't hear it.

"So much for witchcraft," giggled Michelle. "So, tell me how this silly game works, Jerry. I guess if I'm going to be watching it for the rest of my life, I might as well learn the rules." The cough from the conservatory was even fainter this time. It would be.

*Michaele Jordan was born in LA, educated in New York, and lives in Cin-*

*cinnati. She's worked at a kennel, a Hebrew School and AT&T. She's a little odd. Now she writes, supervised by a long-suffering husband and two domineering cats. Her first novel, Blade Light, was serialized in Jim Baen's Universe, followed by her occult thriller, Mirror Maze. Her work has appeared in the "Magazine of Fantasy and Science Fiction" and "Buzzy Mag". Horror fans will enjoy her 'Blossom' series, which appeared in The Crimson Pact, Volumes 4 and 5. Her website is www.michaelejordan.com.*

# THIS WAY TO THE GOATMAN

*By T.L. Beeding*

Are you sure this is safe?"

Kendra struck a match, its actinic flare casting shadows that deepened her annoyed frown. She ignored the question, touching the flame to the wick of the black pillar candle before her.

"It's fine, Lucas. This bridge has been here since the 1800s. The worst that can happen is we get splinters and bit by mosquitos."

Lucas swallowed down the plethora of concerns in his throat, watching her methodically shake out the match. Striking a new one, touching it to the next candle. Then the next. The flickering light grew with each lit wick until they were surrounded by a circle of warmth. It weakly illuminated the graffiti-covered iron trusses to either side, attracting a swarm of curious insects from the stretch of woodland beyond the bridge's crossing. A chill raced down Lucas's spine.

"I meant the ritual."

A heavy sigh blew from Kendra's nose. She hoisted herself to her feet, grabbing the canister of table salt she'd stolen from the kitchen. It cascaded from the spout, drawing a line of white outside the ring of candles encompassing them.

"It's fine. I Googled it."

"Are you *sure*—"

The salt hissed to a stop, leaving the circle partly open near Lucas's side. She shot a glare over her shoulder, brown eyes flashing dangerously in the dancing flames.

"Do you want to sit in the truck, then?" She gestured angrily to the opening in the salt circle. "If so, this is your last chance. Once I close the circle, we're stuck. Nothing can come in or out unless permission is granted."

Lucas stared, unsure of what to do. He considered the gap closely, chewing on his lower lip. Eyes falling across the silhouetted treetops, from which came a grating cacophony of insectile shrieking. He *should* leave, knowing what they were getting themselves into. Despite a history of unexplained occurrences and police reports, their parents had tried their best to discredit the 'nonsense' about the supposed demon of the woods – the Goatman. It was only a myth, they said, invented to keep people from doing stupid things and getting themselves hurt. There was no such thing as a half-man, half-goat that haunted Old Alton Bridge.

But that explanation didn't sit well with everyone else living in Copper Canyon. From what Kendra told him, she'd been cornered in the locker room after declaring she didn't believe in the Goatman. She'd been tormented for daring to speak ill of him, for trying to explain the inexplicable. Dared to prove for herself if the Goatman was real or not. She'd come home like a storm cloud – agitated, brooding, and black and blue. Thundering up the stairs before their parents could see and locking herself in her room. The angry clacking of her keyboard was the only sound she made all night. When she'd finally reappeared later that night, cleaned up and bandaged, she demanded Lucas take a ride with her.

And here they wound up, sitting in the middle of Goatman's Bridge at midnight, in the middle of an abandoned forest. Building a ritual circle. Attempting to summon the demon of the woods.

"I don't think we should be doing this. What if someone catches us?"

"No one's out here. The Goatman *isn't* real." Kendra's eyes narrowed. "And I'm going to prove it to everyone once and for all." She turned back to the gap in the salt circle, tipping the canister. Letting salt waterfall down, closing them in with a complete, solid white line.

A hush fell over the woods – though it could have been because the time-eaten planks rattled beneath the canister as Kendra set it down. The cloud of insects around their candles dispersed, lingering just outside the ring of light. Looping in slow, methodical figures. She settled on the opposite side of the circle, hand reaching for the backpack she brought along. Setting it in her lap and unzipping it. From within she pulled out a flat, rectangular board and set it face-up on the splintered wood between them. Lucas swallowed hard.

"A spirit board?"

"It's the only way to contact a demon, if they actually exist." She retrieved the board's planchette from the bottom of the bag, placing it atop the curved letters and numbers across its shadowy face. Lastly, she held out a compact notebook and pen. "I need you to take notes of what the board says."

Lucas nervously accepted the items, trying not to tremble as Kendra touched the tips of her fingers to the curved bottom of the planchette. Her pink tongue poked between her lips in concentration.

"Are there any spirits with us on this bridge tonight?" She began, voice cutting through the muted hush. A faint echo repeated back, thrumming between the rusted iron trusses. Lucas's already pounding heart skipped a few beats.

"C'mon, Kendra, we should leave..."

"I already told you we *can't*," she cut him off with a scathing glare. "If you were gonna be chicken shit about it, you should have said something earlier."

"You didn't say we were going to Goatman's Bridge!" He squeaked.

Kendra's lips peeled back into an angry snarl. "Of all the people to have my back, it should be *you!* You *know* the whole Goatman thing is bullshit!"

Lucas shoved the notebook off his lap, letting it fall to the planks. The candle flames flickered as he shakily got to his knees. "If you don't believe any of this is real, then why can't we just break the circle and go home?"

"Fine. Go home, then." The sounds of the woods died to near silence at her clipped command. Her eyes smoldered, honey embers in the candlelight. Jaw flexing in pinched anger. "See for yourself what happens when you go back and tell Mom and Dad what we've been doing."

A heavy lump swelled in the back of Lucas's throat. Fear greater than that of the Goatman forced him back into his seat. Dutifully taking the notebook back into his lap. Clearing her throat, Kendra refocused her attention on the board.

"Are there any spirits with us on the bridge tonight?"

The silence continued, leaving them with only flickering shadows.

The burbling creek that snaked below the bridge, once blotted out by the insects, rushed like rapids in the pressing quiet. After a long pause, Lucas dared to look up. Kendra remained focused on the spirit board, chestnut curls framing her face – bringing out the sharpest angles of her hawkish features.

Then her hands began to move. His eyes widened as the planchette scraped across the board in long, elaborate loops.

"Are you doing that?" He asked nervously.

"No." Kendra's eyes followed the planchette as it slowed, coming to rest on the word in the upper left corner.

*Yes.*

"Yes, there's a spirit here?"

The planchette didn't move. Lucas stared at it, watching it quiver beneath Kendra's fingertips, poised like a tiger ready to pounce. The candles sputtered between rapid breaths issuing from her lips. Eyes narrowed, she leaned forward. Staring into the glass eye of the planchette.

"What the hell..." she whispered faintly.

"What is it?" Lucas hissed, leaning forward to see.

Kendra's hands came up, a shriek piercing the silence of the night. Lucas's heart leapt into his throat, choking in a fit of startled coughing. His vision tunneled, adrenaline thrusting his gut into a wave of nausea. He managed to gasp his way out of unconsciousness, only to realize that his sister was giggling.

"That's not funny, Kendra!"

"Of course it's funny," she wiped a tear from her eye, stifling laughter behind her hand. "And of *course* I was moving it the whole time. This shit isn't real, Lucas. And I just proved it to you." She spread her hands to encompass the darkness. The silence that pressed in on all sides. "There's no such thing as the Goatman."

*Clickety-clack, clickety-clack.*

The creaking planks drew a real scream from Kendra's throat this time. A jolt of fright caused her knee to bump the spirit board, shifting the planchette across its face. Lucas caught sight of motion behind her head; a dark figure approached, silhouette barely visible against the moonless backdrop of night. Kendra followed his gaze, whipping over her shoulder. Gasping at the shadow that loomed ever closer.

"Who's there?" she screeched.

The figure slowed as it stepped into the yellowed candlelight. A man looked back at them, dark skin glowing warm in the suffused light. His eyes were dim beneath an old-fashioned straw hat, wrinkled at the corners in weathered crow's feet. He sported a gnarled wooden cane that tapped against the planks as he walked.

"Here now, what's goin' on?" His voice was gentle but booming. Friendly. He looked at Kendra and Lucas in turn. "What're you two doin' out here on a night like this? Shouldn't y'all be at home?"

It took a moment for both to recover from shock. "Uh," Kendra eventually blurted, a hot blush burning pink across her cheeks. "I-I…we…"

The old man glanced at the spirit board, the black candles. At Kendra and Lucas's petrified faces. Then his eyes fell on the salt circle; a smirk tugged one side of his thin lips. Something about it riddled Lucas's chest with anxiety. "Lemme guess – ya'll are trying to make contact with the Goatman, ain't ya?"

"Y-yeah," Kendra sounded mortified.

"I seen many kids like you come out here, tryin' the same thing before. Over'n over'n over again. Ain't nothin' come through for them, o'course." He leaned atop the cane, pointing a gnarled finger at the spirit board. "'Course, ain't none of them had a spirit board, neither."

Lucas glanced at the abandoned planchette. At how, despite Kendra's startled motion as the old man approached, it remained over the word *Yes*.

"Wh-what are *you* doing out here this time of night?" Lucas forced himself to ask.

"Me? I live 'round here." The old man pointed over his shoulder, back toward the darkness he came from. "Right up there, just past the bridge. Ain't nobody usually out here at night, so I come a'walkin' for peace o'mind." A deep chuckle welled up from his chest. "Well, 'course that's different tonight." He nodded to their circle. To the board. "Y'all had any luck with that thing?"

"No," Kendra replied quietly, shaking her head. "It's fake…demons aren't real."

"Well, now, I wouldn't say that." The old man pursed his lips. "There's a lot o'things in this world that can't never be explained. I lived a long time, and to this day I still ain't sure of some'o the things I seen out in these woods. Some'o the things I heard."

"What things?"

"There's sure some demons in these here woods – not just the Goatman, neither." The old man scratched his chin, fingertips scraping against wiry stubble. "I seen many a'wanderin' travelers go into these here woods, havin' yet to come back. Searchin' for somethin' they ain't got no business tryin' to contact. Y'can sometimes hear 'em up and down these trails, hollerin' and crashin' 'round. Wantin' to make themselves heard. To be found. They's the ones that're easy to steer clear of. But the others…" His eyes went dark. "The ones ya *can't* see'n hear are the most dangerous of 'em all. The ones that sneak up on ya, in the dead o'night, with ain't a whisper o'warnin'. One second you're alone, then in the next, they jump ya."

Ice settled in the pit of Lucas's stomach. He glanced at Kendra, whose eyes were wide and nervous. Fixated on the old man. After a long moment of uncomfortable silence, his dark gaze met hers. The smile returned to his wizened lips.

"Y'all ever even used a spirit board before now?"

"N-no." Kendra managed to sputter.

The smile widened, showing nearly all of his yellowed, grimy teeth. "I can show ya how, if ya like."

Lucas cut off Kendra's reply before she could make it – if she even had one. "Where did you say you lived again?" he shakily demanded, clenching trembling fists.

The old man's eyes met his, narrowing. That wide, creepy smile remained frozen to his face. "My apologies, I didn't introduce myself proper-like." A hand fanned across his chest. "The name's Oscar. I live just up north beyond the bridge, like I told ya. Down the path and into the woods a little. I own a farm up thataway. Just a little goat farm, that's all." He stuck a thumb over his shoulder. "Didn't ya see the sign before ya crossed the bridge?"

The siblings shook their heads. Oscar chuckled again. "It's a little hard to see in the dark – 'specially since y'all didn't have yer headlights on."

"How did you know we didn't have our headlights on?" Kendra asked suspiciously.

"Once ya live alone in a place for so long, ya learn to be a little wary of yer surroundin's." He touched the brim of his straw hat with his thumb, pushing it further up above his eyes. He leaned heavily on his cane again. "I only been caught once unawares by someone crossin' without no head-lights. And that was enough fer me." His eyes fell back to the spirit board. "Now, how 'bout that spirit board?"

"It doesn't work," Lucas piped up, starting to get scared. "Demons aren't real, like my sister says."

Oscar slowly shook his head. His smile never faded. "Still ain't con-vinced, is ya?" He rapped the bottom of his cane against the bridge's wooden planks. They rattled in their casings. "Listen. I ain't just some fuddy-duddy what lives by himself in the woods. I ain't got no reason to make up fairy-tales 'bout the things I seen." He pointed to the spirit board again. "I used one o'them many times before, and I guarantee y'all are missin' the key to makin' it work."

"What would that be?" Kendra demanded, beginning to sound like her old self again – annoyed.

"An open mind." Those dark eyes met hers once more. "Let me show ya how to use it. If it ain't gonna work, then you got solid proof that demons are fake. Ain't that right?"

"Yeah, I guess so."

"That's right." Oscar's cane swirled as his hands opened, taking in the salt circle. "Now, may I join y'all?"

"Yeah."

Oscar didn't move right away. Kendra frowned up at him. "Well, what are you waiting for?"

The old man's smile tightened wickedly. "'Course y'know, it ain't proper to allow someone into yer circle without permission. Ya gotta clear a path fer me, that's all."

Every hair on the back of Lucas's neck stood rigid. But before he could protest, Kendra shrugged. Reaching forward, she swept away part of the salt circle – at the toes of Oscar's worn, holey leather boots.

The shrieking of the cicadas and crickets returned, rising up in a swell of thunder. The insects swarming the candlelight evaporated from the bridge in a startled flutter. Lucas's heart dropped into his stomach as Oscar set his cane down and stepped across the salt line, lowering himself to the planks with crossed legs. The candle flames hissed and spat, sending hot black wax dripping across the wood. Oscar didn't seem to notice the wax that rolled onto the cuffs of his trouser legs; he kept his eyes on the spirit board, kept the grin plastered to his weathered face.

"Now, put yer fingertips on that there planchette again," he breathed heavily.

Kendra looked wary but did as she was told. Her fingertips touched the rounded edges of the planchette, bringing it back to the center of the board.

"Ask yer question."

"Are there any spirits on the bridge with us—" Kendra barely got the words out before her hands began flying across the board in long, circular motions. She drew a ragged, terrified gasp. Lucas bit his lower lips so hard he tasted blood. Oscar didn't move at all.

"Stop doing that, Kendra!" he demanded shakily. "I told you it's not funny!"

"It's not me, I *swear*!" she cried, tears welling up in her eyes. They dripped onto the edge of the board as the planchette stopped, then jerked her hands forward and up – to the top left corner.

*Yes.*

"What is this?" Kendra sobbed. Her gaze flew up to Oscar, who sat perfectly still beside them. Dark eyes wide open and focused on the planchette. The grin began to eat his entire face as Kendra's hands were dragged along the board like a rag doll's. "How are you doing that?"

"I told you, there's demons in these here woods." The wicked smile turned on Kendra. Oscar's eyes glowed a diffuse, honey gold as the candle flames grew into hot, sputtering fires. "You just ain't listenin'. No one listens, 'specially when they's crossed into *my* territory."

"*Who are they*?" She pleaded. "Who are the demons?"

The planchette tore across the board. Dragging Kendra's arms along in three, quick jerks.

*YOU*

The ring of flames blew out in a gust of wind. Kendra's scream was silenced in a choked-off, bloody gurgle. Something large and powerful clipped Lucas's left side before he could react, knocking him back across the rotting planks of wood. The back of his head hit a candle, hot wax searing his scalp and clinging to his hair. Panicking, he flipped onto his stomach and pushed himself to hands and knees. Splinters jabbed into his palms as he shoved himself upward, screaming. Running for the truck parked at the entrance of the bridge. He grabbed the door handle and yanked, but it was locked. He slammed a fist against the window, willing it to open. Trying to ignore the scuffling behind him. Too late, the thought crossed his mind that he needed the keys to get in – finally registering that he'd left Kendra behind. Lucas whirled.

*"Kendra!"*

A large, dark blot squirmed in the center of the bridge. Heavy, wet squelching added staccato to the insects echoing Lucas's panic. To the planks of the bridge, which creaked and rattled as the inky blot began to take a shape. It rose on two legs, darker than black, outlined against the moonless night. The straw hat on its head fell away, exposing two thick, short horns that ended in sharp, dagger-like points. Dripping with clots of blood.

"What are you?" Lucas wailed tearfully.

The shape slowly turned. Two, piercing yellow eyes burned like flames in the dark, staring straight ahead. A golden lining to a short snout protruding from an inhuman face. The low growl that emanated from its throat ended in a chuckle, vibrating through the iron trusses in Oscar's voice.

"Didn't ya see the sign, boy?"

The right arm rose, toward the bridge's structure. Lucas followed its direction, to a rust-bitten tin sign hammered into the truss. A sign they hadn't seen when he and Kendra pulled up in the truck with their headlights off, armed only with candles and reckless stupidity. Lucas barely caught its time-rubbed words before the shape pounced, goring his throat with the horns atop its head. Spilling fresh, hot blood across the planks of Old Alton Bridge.

*This way to the Goatman.*

**T.L. Beeding** *is a single mother from Kansas City, MO. She is co-editor of Crow's Feet Journal and Paramour Ink, and is a featured horror author for Black Ink Fiction. When she is not writing, T.L. works at a busy orthopedic hospital, mending broken bones. She can be found on Twitter at @tlbeeding.*

# SWEAT

## By Joshua Bryant

J ohn Laramie felt uncomfortable. It wasn't emotional or mental; he was deeply, excruciatingly, physically uncomfortable. Like he had a tremendous itch that was impossible to scratch. Like he had to desperately go to the bathroom but was terribly constipated. Like he was in the throes of a fever and was just about to fall into delirium.

But despite all of this, he was still at work, his fingers moving along his keyboard with an uninterrupted attitude. All that reflected his torment was the thick beads of sweat that were dripping down his brow, from his armpits, and trickling along his spine. There were dark patches of wetness all over his clothing, from the massive pools that were his armpits down to the rings about his ankles. He kept wiping sweat from his eyes and pouring small amounts of baby powder into the palms of his hands.

Darlene in the cubicle across from John kept looking over at him. She had a look of disgust stamped onto her face so obvious it was almost cruel. Yet, John did not notice her. He simply carried on typing, inputting data, and performing his duties. He was oblivious to anything except his work and his discomfort. The rest of the world could have been consumed in fire for all John knew. Darlene, on the other hand, was so distracted by the sight of him that she was becoming incredibly distressed.

She leaned across her desk and squirted hand sanitizer into her palm. She scrubbed it vigorously into her skin, wondering whether there was enough distance between to keep her air clean of whatever it was that was affecting him. She watched him, shaking her head at the sight. He looked like he might keel over any second. She hoped he didn't. The sight of dead things always made Darlene sick.

John took his hands away from his keyboard for just a moment to violently scratch his neck and forehead. He looked at his fingers after doing so and made a strange face. He wiped whatever he had seen on his pants and then continued working.

Darlene looked at the spot on his pants where he had just wiped his hand. She could see something there, like a thin line of glistening saliva or mucus. She looked away from it to keep from gagging. She tried to continue working but found it too much of a struggle. She had to keep looking at him.

It wasn't just the sweat that lathered him from head to toe that was so engrossing, it was also the diligence with which he was still accomplishing work. He was like a machine! His hands moving with such rigorous power all about his keyboard. His eyes, unblinking and blood shot, staring in an uninterrupted line at his computer screen. And Darlene knew his mind must be awash with numbers and calculations, like some sentient calculator.

She hated him for that. Every day of the work week he was there before anybody else, and he was always the last to clock out. He seemed to be a part of that office, as much as the printer or the air conditioner. She had been here longer than him by two years, but still he was the one getting raises, he was the one the boss bragged on. But now, looking at him, Darlene could finally smile.

It was a smile of satisfaction, a curl of her lips that was neither joyful nor laughing. It was a smile reserved for when people see their enemy humiliated.

She squirted more sanitizer into her hand and chuckled to herself. There the great hard worker was, sweating like a whore in a church, she thought. Working himself to death.

She looked over again to find him scratching his face once more. He was leaving long red streaks in his skin. He wiped more sticky fluid onto his pants. Darlene couldn't help but laugh aloud. Of course, John didn't hear her.

Hours passed, and while Darlene watched John sweat continuously, scratch himself with greater intensity, obviously becoming increasingly uncomfortable, her personal satisfaction grew and grew.

At lunch time, John stayed at his desk and Darlene took a few moments to stand up and look down at him like a triumphant soldier. Sitting with her friends in the cafeteria she told them with a bright smile on her face: "There really is justice in the world."

When she returned, Darlene was prepared to continue her silent gloating, but what she saw caught her breath in her throat. John was sitting upright in his chair, his hands clean of baby powder, his eyes moist and healthy looking, and his skin was completely devoid of sweat. Even his clothes were dry. He looked up at her and smiled genuinely.

"For a second there I thought I was going to have to go home!" he was saying. "But, geez, lying in bed doesn't pay the bills, am I right? Guess I sweated it out though."

Darlene was shaking with fury. She slammed herself into her seat and began pummeling the keyboard with her fingers, not caring if the work was accurate or not. She didn't look back over at John for some time.

Near the end of the day, she decided to send a hateful look over at him, but instead a cup, placed upside down on his desk, caught her attention. It was his coffee cup, but she had never seen it placed in such a way before. It was like he had captured a fly within it, but some inner intuition was telling her it was more than a mere insect.

Every now and then, John would scoot the cup a little farther away from himself and then dab his forehead with frantic fingers, as if searching for something. Darlene was thoroughly interested. She let the rest of the day slip by, her eyes looking with growing hunger for whatever was hidden beneath John's cup.

The end of the day came and everybody got up from their desks, preparing to go home. Darlene got up as she always did, watching John from the corners of her eyes. He shut down his computer and reached for the cup with a trembling hand.

"So, John!" Darlene said, leaning on his desk. He looked up at her, his hand retreating from the cup. "I was wondering if you would want to go out for drinks tonight with me and Cindy. You know, it's just I'd like to see more of you."

John's mouth fell open and his eyes were wide. Darlene knew he had completely forgotten about the cup. She allowed herself a smile of satisfaction.

"S-sure!" he said, standing up and fumbling with his jacket like a little boy. Darlene walked with him to the punch-out machine, smiling and joking, but always looking over her shoulder to where she knew his cubicle to be.

"Oh shoot!" she said when they were getting into the elevator to go down to the lobby. "I forgot my car keys at my desk, would you mind meeting me at the bar? I'll try to be quick."

John smiled at her and blushed. "Yeah, of course!"

She watched the elevator doors slide shut. He waved to her happily just before they disappeared from one another's sight. Darlene turned about quickly and whispered to herself, "What an idiot."

She walked past the empty cubicles, her high heels making resounding knocks on the carpeted floor. Her pace was eager, for some reason she couldn't understand; she felt like she was going to uncover some dark secret. Something that John Laramie didn't want her, or anyone else to know, and the knowledge that she was going to find out what that was made her feel a deep sense of gratification.

She stopped at his dark cubicle and turned the computer monitor on for a small amount of light. There the ceramic mug sat, upside down, concealing something. Darlene licked her lips eagerly.

With a shaking hand she slowly reached for the cup. Her heart was racing with adrenaline, her stomach pulsing with the joyous fear of a child stealing candy. Her fingers curled about the cup, and she pulled it upward with a small hiss of breath.

She froze, her eyes wide, her mouth slightly open. She didn't know what she was looking at. It wasn't a bug, though it was surely the size of one. It didn't move or scurry away, it actually simply looked up at her with a puzzling expression. It was a tiny, naked John Laramie.

"What the fu-" She began to say and then she was falling backwards, screaming.

The tiny John had leaped with surprising speed onto her arm and was now climbing up her sleeve. She fell onto the floor, clawing and swatting at where she felt his little body squirming along her skin. She wasn't screaming, but she was grunting and swearing in a high-pitched, frantic voice. No matter how much she pummeled herself, she couldn't stop his tickling movements. Finally, in desperation, she ripped her sleeve off and flung the tattered cloth away from her.

In the dim light she looked and looked for the insect-sized person. At first she couldn't find him, in fact, she couldn't even feel him anymore. Then, in the soft flesh of her inner elbow, she saw a miniscule movement. She stood up and slammed her arm down in front of the computer screen for better light. She looked at her flesh, holding her breath behind clenched teeth.

She saw a little naked leg kicking and squirming as it was making its way into one of her pores. She screamed now and tried to grasp the tiny appendage with pinching fingers. But it escaped into her skin before she could get a hold of it.

"No no no! Oh God, no!" She shouted as she slumped to the floor scratching fearfully at her skin.

After almost an hour of clawing at her arm until it bled, Darlene finally gave up. She cried a little to herself before springing up and racing to the elevator. She was thinking of going to the hospital, but as she waited for the elevator to arrive she thought better of it.

What self-respecting doctor would believe that some tiny person had crawled into her skin? No, she'd be carted off to the psych ward without a second thought.

So, like a hollow woman, she returned home. She didn't notice the drive; all she could think of was the little monstrous John that was somewhere in her body. She didn't know what to do, so she entered her home, bandaged up her arm, took a powerful painkiller, and slunk off to bed.

The next day, she woke up to the raucous beeping of her alarm clock. But she didn't rise. She couldn't. Her sheets were soaked with sweat, her head was throbbing, her stomach was boiling, her body was aching.

Darlene Mathers felt uncomfortable.

*Joshua Bryant* *is a speculative fiction writer from the American Southwest. He prides himself on being an individual and strives to create stories that are just as unique. He is currently working as a cowboy in west Texas, but will stop at nothing to become a full-time writer.*

# 1, 2, (SKIP A FEW) 99, 100.

## By Stephen McQuiggan

**M**y first instinct, as usual in such circumstances, was to cheat. Well, more a blurring of the moral lines than outright skulduggery, but you get the general idea. A little bending of the rules, I'm declared the victor, and no one gets hurt. Oh, and of course, the overwhelming sense of satisfaction of getting one over on a group of people I had nothing but contempt for.

How I ended up in Tulip Botley's country home (a *retreat* no less) was a mystery that baffled me, even as I sat sipping cocktails on her voluminous lawn. I didn't know her or any of her chinless friends and bony chested admirers who gabbled around me in the flapping marquee next to the sprawling pile she laughingly referred to as the 'Cottage'.

I was a council estate lad, born and bred (and borne on bread) with no earthly right to be there, save to mend the plumbing or trim the topiary. Yet there I sat, shackled by a starched collar, wearing a hired suit so luxurious I couldn't help but scan it for lint at every available opportunity. And yet I congratulated myself. Whilst my peers had chased easy money and easier girls, I had educated myself, making myself faster and fitter for the hunt of better things.

Jesson was the reason I had been invited, but Jesson had cried off sick at the last minute. So there I was, clutching a tall glass of Pym's, filled up like a fruit basket, attempting to talk without moving my mouth lest my heritage be discovered and I wound up being put in the stocks. It started to rain, great fat goblets of gentrified country water splashing demurely from the fairy lights, when Tulip finally confronted me.

"Where's Jesson?" she asked, her eyebrows suggesting I had done away with him. She was holding a goldfish bowl of Tanqueray, twiddling her necklace, its huge ruby dangling like a devil's teardrop. "How is it you know him again?"

"I met him in his Club." I didn't add that I tended bar there and that, after extracting a rather drunken Jesson from a number of scrapes, he had adopted me as a sort of working class mascot, and invited me here as a nod to his own twisted sense of humour.

"I thought perhaps you schooled with him."

"No." I kept my answers clipped. The schoolyards I had run in were definitely free of Jesson and his ilk.

Tulip smiled, the kind of smile that suggested she knew my secret but was content to let me carry on my little charade for the time being. "He's probably nursing the nanny of all hangovers," she said, mock petulantly.

I returned her smile. I was on safer ground here. "He was pretty tight when I saw him last," I agreed. "So, this is your parents' place?"

"One of them; a quaint little holiday home for their leisure pursuits. I use it frequently myself. It's so nice to be out of the city, free from its rules, don't you think?"

I ignored her question. I knew only my own rules. "Your parents abroad then?"

"No, Papa's still here," she laughed with a wicked musicality. "I guess part of him will always be. He's asleep though, that's why we're outside. He can be such a grump if he's woken prematurely. You come all the way down by yourself, I gather. I didn't notice your car..."

That was because I caught the train and trudged the last four miles down a maze of winding lanes.

"My driver left me off. I'd planned to return with Jesson."

"We'll arrange a lift for you," Tulip said, frowning as the rain picked up. The marquee flapped like a gossip's tongue and all the lights momentarily dimmed. "The weather can be such a bore." She sounded genuinely disgusted, as if some sugar daddy god had promised her sunshine and let her down at the last minute. "We'll have to go inside."

"Nonsense," I said, trying on haughty and liking the feel of it until a great blam of thunder knocked it out of me. The rain fell in heavy glass sheets and covered my blushes.

I watched them all hurry indoors, save for a few brave ones who scurried off to lower the hoods of their dinky little convertibles. My anxiety began to gnaw at me again—under the cottage's roof, no matter how big and spacious it was, I would be captive to scrutiny, unable to wander off amid the laburnums and rhododendrons, and easy prey to all the usual interrogations posing as innocent inquiries.

The life was sucked out of the throng as soon as it found a roof over its head, all the aimless chat and mundane self-reflection washed away by the downpour. They murmured testily as they sized each other up at close quarters.

"What now?" Tulip asked her fawning acolytes, in the manner of one addressing the survivors of Armageddon. "Have you brought your trusty viola, Tristram? A feisty concerto would be just the thing. Nothing *too* boisterous, mind. We can't go waking Papa; he's a terror when he's roused."

Tristram, a lanky man with a tie thicker than his torso, shook his head in shame.

"Perhaps you know of some diversion?" She turned to me, a wicked little glint in her eye. "What do you and Jesson do to pass the weary hours at that club of yours?"

I was on the verge of suggesting bludgeoning some spoilt trust-fund brats but took a drink instead to buy myself some thinking time. "What about a game of Hide and Seek?" I offered up, half in jest, to these ridiculous overgrown children.

It was the old oak dresser planted by the fireplace that had put the idea into my head.

It was so similar to the one in my aunt Nora's ramshackle old farmhouse – a place I'd spent most of my childhood in, running amok with my ever expanding horde of feral cousins, playing Tag and Cowboys and Indians and, when it rained, Hide and Seek. I used to hide in the oak dresser and not one of my relatives ever had the gumption to sniff me out.

There was a smattering of laughter, amused and incredulous, and I took another drink to fortify myself. It was too late to retract now, I'd have to brazen it out. I fully expected Tulip to scythe me down with a sneer, but instead she positively beamed.

"How delightfully gauche," she trilled, and for a moment I saw beneath the vanity that wealth afforded her and thought her beautiful.

Their host's enthusiasm was all her guests needed to change their tune. Suddenly, I was being slapped on the back and declared 'a good egg' by all and sundry. There's nothing these idle layabouts love more than some ironic tackiness. It allows them to feel superior without having to lift a finger to earn it.

"You'll be the Seeker, of course," Tulip informed me, caressing my cheek with one jewel encrusted hand, cold as a mummy's, with all its attendant finery of the tomb. "We'll have to think up a special reward for you, if you manage to find *me*." She winked like one long out of practice in the art of subtlety, her eyes gleaming as red as the ruby round her neck.

I smiled politely, unsure how to take her blatant come-on—girls like her were used to being fawned over. It might be highly amusing, I thought, to see her face when I turned her down flat. As for being the Seeker, I would have insisted upon it myself. What better opportunity to have a nose around the place than the pretext of a stupid party game?

I chuckled inwardly as all the Bartholomews and Sebastians, all the Merediths and Sashas, fled from the room to find a hidey hole; they sounded like hyperactive kids, jacked on candy, and it was easy to imagine their laughter playing on a loop in the elevators of Hell. Tulip was the last to leave. She fingered her necklace by the doorway, the ruby penduluming back and forth in a hypnotic red blur. She looked me up and down, nodded her pointy little chin in satisfaction, and then exited in a swish of soft fabric.

"Make sure you count the full hundred," she admonished on her way out.

I'd never counted the full hundred in my life, and I always peeked —like I said before, I'm a habitual cheat. I gave them just enough time to scurry into their lairs and sighed contentedly. I'd no intention of finding them anytime soon, not now I had the run of the place; who knew what secrets I could unearth, what trinkets I could pocket.

I made my way to the downstairs bathroom first, hoping that none of those inbred toffs had hidden there, with the idea of procuring some quality pharmaceuticals—these well-heeled types were synonymous with neuroses, and their private docs were generous with their scripts.

The bathroom was so lavish I fully expected to find a Visitor's Book by the mother of pearl towel rack. I found no pills, no uppers or downers or inbetweeners. Whatever little helpers Tulip relied on were stashed from prying eyes. Disappointed, I decided to check the downstairs out more thoroughly.

The kitchen was huge, full of all kinds of gadgets and gizmos. It looked like a showroom in one of those *Ideal Home* catalogues and I doubted if a single onion had ever been chopped, or a rind of bacon ever sizzled in that pristine cavern.

My search threw up nothing of note, save for a pinkie finger holding closed a cupboard door beneath the sink, so I made good my retreat before I accidentally stumbled across some contortionist college boy holding his scented breath. As I passed by the cellar door I stopped to give it a try.

I fully expected it to be locked, but it opened with a well-oiled click and I felt my heart beat a little faster; surely there would be some bottles of *Chateau Pretension 56*, or a nice cask of *Ostentation 42* down there. I could flog any dusty wine I found there at the Club, and make a tidy packet into the bargain.

I flicked the light on, a cheery whistle sticking in my throat as I glanced down at the first step leading down into the dank chill. A necklace lay pooled there, its Devil eye ruby pendant winking wickedly up at me in the sterile, fluorescent glare. So, Tulip was down there. I admired her competitive streak—it may be just a 'gauche' party game but she was still desperate to win.

I placed the necklace in my pocket and inched my way, oh so quietly, down the stairs. I'd decided there and then that she would be the first to be caught. It would ruin her evening if nothing else.

The light only illuminated the top few risers. By the time I was half-way down I was in total darkness, the door behind and above, shining like some celestial portal. I was thinking of retracing my steps before I tripped and broke my neck when I heard the faint muffle of voices and saw a weak, pale light, like the onset of a migraine, blurring in the distance.

So, Tulip had brought a few of her acolytes down here with her, maybe the whole damn lot of them. I pondered locking the cellar door and heading back to the city in one of their convertibles, but the idea of wiping the smugness off their pointy faces made me carry on.

The further I walked, the more confused I became. The corridor seemed to stretch for miles, a veritable labyrinth hewn through the bedrock the cottage was built on. Was Tulip a budding Bond villain? Had her parents constructed a dungeon for some high society sex games far from prying eyes?

I followed the murmurs, buzzing in the dim light like a nest of soporific hornets, as my mind conjured ever more bizarre scenarios. The corridor turned abruptly, and I found myself in a huge natural chamber filled with firelight from a rock edged pit. Around the flames, quaffing their cocktails, stood Tulip and her guests, looking every bit at home as if they were chewing the fat at some local gala or ball.

"Ah, there you are at last!" Tulip declared, as I stumbled in, still squinting after my journey through the murk. I clutched the necklace in my pocket and plastered on a diffident smile. "We were beginning to think we were going to have to look for *you*."

I was busy rehearsing a spontaneous retort when Jesson stepped out of the crowd, brandy glass held at a rakish angle, and said, "I told you he was resourceful, didn't I?"

"What the fuck are you doing here?" I asked, all the refinement seeping from my voice; in the echoing chamber, I sounded like a stereotypical tradesman. "I thought you were sick."

"I've been accused of that many times," Jesson smiled.

"You didn't *really* believe he would invite you here," Tulip laughed into her dainty hand. "Seriously? A common pleb like you?"

"But he did ... he ..." The cavern multiplied their mocking laughter and I floundered.

"Not invited," Jesson corrected me, "*lured*."

"Is this some kind of joke?" I could tell by their cruel, eager faces that if it was then it was most certainly on me.

"Normally Jesson brings us some true down and outs, homeless types soaked in meths and cheap wine, but as it's Papa's birthday he promised us all something a teensy bit more refined." Tulip leaned over and gave Jesson's pencil neck a predatory lick. "Though you're dumb as a bum—we didn't even have to trick you into coming down here. Such a fortuitous game you picked—Papa's so fond of Hide and Seek."

"Maybe we should talk about this back upstairs," I said jovially, backing away, hoping to disarm them with charm before legging it. "You said yourself you didn't want to wake your old dad."

They were following me en masse, mirroring my every step, backing me into a corner.

"Oh, but Papa's wide awake now," Tulip said, "and I'm sure he'd love to play with you." She rushed toward me, nothing but hatred in her angular face, and I felt the stab of her nails through my rented shirt. Her spittle splashed my eyes as she screamed out, "You're IT!" and pushed.

I toppled backward, expecting to crack my skull on the rough rock floor but I just kept on falling. When the ground finally rushed up to punch the air from me, I found myself in darkness. Above me, staring down from a circular star, Tulip, Jesson, and the others peered at me like I was some crippled exhibit in Bedlam.

I heard panting to my left, an eager doglike sound, and I struggled to my feet. The darkness disappeared for a moment as great flashes of pain scythed across my vision. I squinted up, hoping against all reason that Jesson would be dangling a rope down to me, but the only thing he cast down was his trademark sneer.

"Okay, joke's over," I shouted up. The panting was drawing nearer, reverberating off the craggy walls of my pit before stopping abruptly. Two red eyes shone out of the darkness across from me, red as the ruby in the necklace in my pocket. A figure emerged from the shadow, stood on the dim border of the light so that I had to strain to see—but what I saw was enough to start *me* panting.

It was a hideous, shrivelled thing; a homunculus stitched from leather, with razor ribs and crow beak claws and thin dripping fangs. Its eyes reflected back the firelight from above as if lit from within by ancient malice. I backed myself away into a wall as a warm spray of urine splashed down my thigh.

"Papa loves to play, don't you Papa?" Tulip called down, and the thing in the shadows grunted in gurgling agreement. "He especially loves Hide and Seek. He reckons it makes the meat more tender."

I inched my way along the wall as my eyes grew accustomed to the dark. I could make out at least three tunnels on this side of the pit and could feel the cold, fetid air flowing up from their depths.

"Off you go," Tulip urged me, "Papa will count you down before he comes looking. Oh, and never fret, he's *very* meticulous about the rules." A gentle rain of sarcastic laughter fell down upon me as the thing in the shadows cleared its throat.

"One...two..." it began in a sandpaper rasp, "Skip a few...ninety-nine...one hundred!"

So much for the rules; Papa was a cheat, just like me.

I fled down the nearest tunnel, the whole corridor lit by an eldritch fug, taking every other turn that I came to, until I found myself totally lost. Papa was a cheat, but he was no match for me.

And so here I am, squashed into a niche in the bowels of the earth, speaking with you, my friend. I can see your malevolent eyes, gleaming like the ruby in my pocket, Mr Rat. I take it you *are* a rat—no offence meant, but I'm quite fond of rats; I have been called one often enough. We are vermin brethren you and I, hunted down because of our refusal to be downtrodden, hated for our ability to survive. Has my tale not taught you that?

Perhaps you could show me the way out, my reviled little brother? I promise you a great bounty if you'll only give up the secrets of this lair.

What was that?

Tell me that was *you* that was sniffing, Mr Rat, and grunting so. I don't care if you're lying (I'm a liar myself), just don't tell me it's what I think it is. Adieu, my rodent friend, I must be going again. I leave this necklace in your keeping, for I fear it carries her scent. If you happen to cross my path again, I give you my blessing to gnaw on my bones.

*Stephen McQuiggan* was the original author of the bible; he vowed never to write again after the publishers removed the dinosaurs and the spectacular alien abduction ending from the final edit. His other, lesser known, novels are A Pig's View Of Heaven and Trip A Dwarf.

# ACKNOWLEDGEMENT

The Vanishing Point Magazine would never have come to be without the tireless work of our editorial staff. Thank you very much to Corey Godare, Jacob LeGrand, Amy Orr, and Joseph Peterson.

Thank you very much to all of the writers who shared their work with us. Your imagination is inspiring.

Also thank you to the reader. We hope to see you back for issue #2.

Printed in Great Britain
by Amazon